THE TWIN FLAME RESOLUTION

Also by Michelle Gordon:

Fiction
The Girl Who Loved Too Much

Earth Angel Series
The Earth Angel Training Academy
The Earth Angel Awakening
The Other Side
The Twin Flame Reunion
The Twin Flame Retreat
The Twin Flame Resurrection
The Twin Flame Reality
The Twin Flame Rebellion
The Twin Flame Reignition
The Twin Flame Resolution
The Old Soul's Handbook

Visionary Collection
Heaven dot com
The Doorway to PAM
The Elphite
I'm Here

Children's Fiction
The Magical Faerie Door

Poetry
Duelling Poets

Non-fiction
Where's My F**king Unicorn?

THE TWIN FLAME RESOLUTION

MICHELLE GORDON

First published in Great Britain in 2018 by The Amethyst Angel

ISBN: 978-1-912257-10-2

First Edition

This book is for all my beautiful Faerie God Children -

Tabitha, Dominic, Thomas, Frances,
Sam, Oliver, Walter & Poppy.

I love you all, and I hope the world you grow up in will be
worthy of your light.

PROLOGUE

"You want us to do *what*?"

Magenta smiled at the two Angels, whose mouths were open with shock, and their features conveyed their utter confusion.

"I know, it's a lot to ask of you, and believe me, it's no small task. But I promise I do not ask it of you lightly."

"But, but, but..." Emerald stammered. "*Everything?*" She looked at Mica, who was also apparently lost for words.

Magenta nodded. "Everything. You've seen the way the world is, and you've seen the way things have worked out. You both know, all too well, that it's not the best possible outcome for Earth and her inhabitants."

Mica frowned before finding his voice. "We do know, and you're right. But this is not simply nudging here and there, as we did from the Angelic Realm, this would mean that everything would be different, if we were to comply."

"It is the only way we are going to experience the Golden Age." Magenta smiled. "If you need to be convinced, I will show you what I saw."

Emerald and Mica nodded, and Magenta waved her

hand towards the lake, making the water ripple slightly. In a rapid montage style, the two Angels watched the new fate of the world play out. When the lake went clear again, they looked at Magenta.

"It's beautiful," Emerald whispered. "But are you sure that we cannot get there from where we are? Violet's movie just came out, people are beginning to wake up..."

Magenta shook her head. "It's too little, too late. I have Seen the vision of where the world is currently headed, and it is not good enough."

"I assume it is the vision that we have Seen too. Though, as you were there, on Earth in that vision, I can only assume you have now changed it irrevocably anyway?" Mica commented.

"Indeed," Magenta said. "I do not know the exact details of what you need to do, but I know, without a shadow of a doubt, that you are the Angels for the job. That you will instinctively know what needs to change, and what the Earth Angels need to learn to bring about the new Golden Age you have just witnessed. And I also know that Velvet will listen to you. You may have to say you are from a higher dimension to pull rank a little, but I doubt she, or anyone else, will question it."

The three looked up suddenly, at the sound of someone walking across the pebbles nearby. They waited until the Angel had moved on before continuing their discussion. Magenta looked at the still lake again, and wondered how everyone was coping with her death. She desperately wanted to check in on Steve, but her mission was more important in that moment. She needed Emerald and Mica to accept her proposal before she lost herself in reminiscences of her time with her Flame.

"Steve is doing okay," Emerald said softly, following her gaze. "Everyone has rallied around to support him. And Violet dedicated the movie to you."

Tears filled Magenta's eyes and she nodded. She dried her eyes with her sleeve and returned her determined gaze to the two Angels. "I left everything and everyone I love to ensure that this happens. Because I know that this is my ultimate purpose. To finally move the world into the Golden Age. But I need your help."

Emerald and Mica exchanged a long look.

"Are you certain about the Twin Flames? Must it really be changed that much?"

"Yes," Magenta said firmly. "As you Saw in the vision, in order for the world to shift and Awaken, the Flames must never reunite, or even remember their connection." Magenta saw tears rolling down Emerald's cheeks.

"Our mission was always to reunite the Flames," the Angel whispered. "And you are now giving us the mission of making sure they don't even know each other exists?"

Magenta reached out to touch the Angel's arm. "It's the only way," she said softly. "And as much as I love Steve, and I enjoyed our time together on Earth, it stopped us from fully realising our true power, from living our purpose. Besides," she said, picking up a pebble and smoothing her thumb over the rough surface. "It's not as though the Flames will never have reunited, they have had their time together."

"But if we do this, then they won't remember that they did?" Mica asked.

Magenta shook her head. "No, they won't."

There was a long silence, punctuated only by the whispers of Angels floating towards them on the breeze.

"I trust you," Emerald said finally. "And I know that

Velvet trusts you. So if you say this is what needs to happen, then," she took a deep breath and glanced at Mica, who nodded. "Then we shall do as you ask. We shall go back in time, and change everything."

Magenta smiled. "Thank you."

*   *   *

"Are you absolutely sure about this?"

Emerald looked at Mica, the mist swirling around them as they stood on the edge of the Angelic Realm. "I could see the truth in Magenta's eyes, hear it in her voice. And you Saw the vision…" her voice trailed off and she sighed. "It's not as though the Flames haven't had the lives together they wished for, because they have." She sounded as though she were trying to convince herself as much as her Flame.

"But they won't remember. It will be as though it never happened," Mica said, a pained look on his face, as his hand gripped hers a little tighter.

Emerald glanced around to check they were alone. "Don't you remember?" she whispered, leaning closer to him. "When Velvet went back in time, everyone had visions of what had happened, everyone remembered."

Mica's eyes widened. "So you are hoping the same will happen again? That they will remember what happened anyway? Despite all the changes we make?"

Emerald smiled. "Yes, I am. I mean, I will do as Magenta has asked, but I am praying for a glimmer of the memories to be retained, for them to know that they did in fact get to be with their Flames."

"But will the plan work if that happens?"

Emerald shrugged. "There is nothing we can do about the outcome. All we can do is play our parts to the best of our abilities.”

Mica nodded. “You are right.” He kissed her. “You are always right.”

Emerald chuckled. “And don’t you forget it.”

“So how do we do this?”

“Magenta has gifted us the Old Soul Magick, so we should be able to walk into the mists, and just hold the intention to go back.”

Mica took a deep breath and straightened his shoulders. “Well,” he said, turning to face the mists. “Shall we?”

Emerald tightened her grip around his hand. “Yes, let’s.”

They walked forward, and within a few steps, the mists were so dense they could no longer see, so they both closed their eyes.

CHAPTER ONE
(Take Three)

"Grow, beautiful souls, grow," the little green Faerie whispered, as she worked on her patch of grass in the Elemental Realm.

No matter how slow the growth, and how minutely the grass progressed each day, she loved to help it, to nurture it, to watch it thrive and flourish. It was her duty as a Faerie, as an Elemental on this strange planet called Earth.

She could feel the energy of the grass as it stretched itself just a little more, becoming just a little taller than it was the day before. She smiled, her work was done. Good job too, because her stomach was rumbling and it was definitely time for her tea.

She flew up over the grass, and made her way back to the base of the tree where she had created her home in a small hollow. She greeted the various bugs who lived nearby along the way.

"Good evening, Lucinda," she said to the woodlouse. "Evening, Annie," she said to the ant.

She entered her home and frowned when she found it empty. She hadn't seen Larry all day. Where had that ladybug gone? She shook her head and smiled, no doubt he would be back later, with many tall tales of heroic acts to regale her with.

She went over to her acorn pot, where she had made a stew of berries the day before. She lifted the bark lid and stuck her hand inside, scooping out a handful, before replacing the lid. Eating the berries from her hand, she flew to her twig chair and sat down, her wings resting behind her.

It had been a good day. As had all her days. The sun was shining, her grass had grown, there was enough moisture in the soil, and she felt a deep contentment in her work.

Sure, she would have liked to have had a few more Faerie friends, she did feel a little lonely at times. Even though Larry visited her daily, and Annie and Lucinda were around a lot, they couldn't go flying with her, or catch the Sparrow Express to go on adventures. But she found it difficult to relate to the other Faeries. They thought she was slow and stupid, and took too long to understand simple things.

It wasn't that she was stupid, she was just easily distracted.

"Larry!" she exclaimed, as her friend entered her home. She held out her berry-covered hand. "Made it yesterday."

Larry approached her and swiped her hand with his delicate digit.

She smiled as his energy lit up. She knew he'd like it.

"So where are you been all day?" she asked. "Up to mischief I'm guessing?"

She raised an eyebrow at his silence. "Uh huh, can't even tell me about it, eh? Never mind." She licked her hand clean, then stretched. "I need to get some rest. Today was quite tiring for some reason. Though it was an awesome day. Did you see how blue the sky was? I love it when there are no clouds."

Without waiting for a reply, she kissed the ladybug on his shell then flew to her hammock made of spider's web. Her friend, Charlotte, had made it for her, and it was incredibly snug, with feathers inside from Winnie, her wren friend, to make it nice and warm.

She landed in the hammock and settled down, making it sway slightly as she did so. She loved the feeling of being rocked, it made her feel safe and loved, as though being rocked to sleep by her mother. Not that she remembered being rocked by her mother, but she imagined that it would have felt like this.

Like home.

*   *   *

"Yes, Beryl?" Velvet looked up at the wall, as the sound of wind chimes alerted her to a message from her secretary.

"Hello, Velvet, sorry to disturb you while you are going through the schedules for the new class, but I have two visitors here to see you."

Velvet frowned. "Visitors? Who are they?"

"They are Oracles from the Thirteenth Dimension."

Velvet's eyes widened in confusion. "From the Thirteenth Dimension? Thirteenth? I didn't even know... My goodness, what are they doing here?"

Beryl shook her head. "They wish to speak with you directly. May I send them in?"

Velvet glanced around her office, but she needn't have worried, it was as clean and organised as it always was. "Yes, of course, please send them in."

Beryl nodded and her face faded away. Moments later,

there was a brief knock at the door, and Velvet called out for them to enter. When she saw the two souls who came in, her first instinct was to rise up, and to bow her head to them. They were dressed in the most magnificent robes, which appeared to have been made from stars. They both glowed with auras so bright, it was hard to look at them directly.

"Welcome," Velvet said, when she raised her head. She clicked her fingers and two chairs appeared, which looked almost like thrones, because Velvet was in awe of their majestic grace.

The female Oracle smiled. "Thank you for meeting with us, apologies for arriving unannounced." She moved towards Velvet and embraced her warmly. Velvet was a little surprised at the touch, and for a brief moment, she closed her eyes. The familiarity of the hug puzzled her. She shook hands with the male Oracle.

When they were all seated, Velvet smiled at her guests. "I must say, I have never met Oracles from the Thirteenth Dimension before." She had never even *heard* of the Thirteenth Dimension before, but she wasn't about to admit that. "Please tell me, what brings you here to my Academy?"

The two souls glanced at each other. "First, please allow me to introduce ourselves," the male Oracle said. "I am Miracle, and this is Emergence. And we are powerful Seers. We are Oracles who have been able to See the most likely outcome for Earth, and all the souls who dwell upon her."

Velvet frowned. "We have Seers here, and I do consult with them often. Surely they would know what is to come?"

Emergence shook her head. "The Seers here in the Fifth Dimension, though gifted, are only seeing part of the bigger picture. Whereas we have access to the picture in its entirety. And we realised, that without our presence here at the Academy at this time, the outcome would not be the best for everyone concerned."

"So you have come here to help?" Velvet asked, feeling confused and also perplexed.

"Yes. We have come here to ask if we may become professors. To teach the Earth Angel trainees the essential skills they will need if we are to take the Earth into the Diamond Age."

Velvet saw Miracle glance at Emergence, and thought he looked a little confused, but he said nothing. "The Diamond Age?" Velvet asked. "Whatever is that?"

"It is the age of peace, health, love and respect for all on planet Earth. It is what we wish to Awaken the humans for."

The truth rang out in Emergence's words, and Velvet found herself slightly mesmerised by her passion. "That sounds incredible. How do you know this is possible? Have you experienced it before?"

Emergence shook her head. "No, we have not. But we know it is possible, because *you* will be the one to lead the Earth Angels to it."

Velvet's eyebrows shot up. "Me? I am? On Earth?"

"Yes, Velvet. It is time for you to return to Earth, it is your destiny."

* * *

Starlight frowned at the images flashing before her eyes, wondering why they were so dramatically different to those she had seen not long before.

"What in heaven's name is going on?" she muttered.

She watched and analysed the images at lightning speed, and her confusion grew. "This is... this cannot be..." she muttered.

"But it is."

Starlight spun around at the sound of the angelic voice. She saw a gleaming soul before her, their robes glittering in the moonlight.

"Who are you?" she asked.

"I am Miracle. Oracle from the Thirteenth Dimension."

His voice rang out clearly, but Starlight frowned. "I've not heard of such a dimension? I thought there were just seven?"

Miracle smiled. "There is much in the Universe that is unknown, even to you, Starlight, Angel of Destiny."

Starlight's frown deepened. "You have changed things. This is not how it was meant to be," she said, waving her hand at the fast moving images, scrolling across the clouds behind her.

"Indeed. Much is now different to the future you have foreseen. We have Seen the outcome that you were working towards, and we have come here to ensure that a different path is followed. To the Diamond Age."

Starlight eyes widened. "What is that? I have heard of the Golden Age, but not the Diamond."

"It is the age of true peace, of resilience and respect. It is what can be achieved if you listen to me, and if you comply."

Starlight felt a resistance to his words. She was the Angel of Destiny, it was her mission to lead the world, who was he to tell her what to do?

"We know the Diamond Age is possible," he said softly, as though sensing her doubt. "And we know you are instrumental in making it happen. But you need to trust us."

"Us?" Starlight repeated. "Who else is with you?"

"My fellow Oracle, Emergence, is with me at the Academy, where we will be working with Velvet," Miracle replied.

"Velvet?" Starlight repeated. "You are working with my sister? She has agreed to this?"

"Yes, she has. Though she is unaware of the original course. She is simply being guided by us towards the best possible path."

Starlight folded her arms. Though he emanated love and peace, she could tell that there was much that this Oracle was not sharing with her, and it irked her a little. Why did he not trust her?

"We trust that you will do what is right by the world, and not what you feel pulled towards in this moment," Miracle said, making Starlight think that he could indeed hear her thoughts.

"And how do I know that you are doing right by the world? How do I know that you are not just serving yourself?"

Miracle chuckled. "Because myself and Emergence are Oracles, we do not know how to serve only ourselves. It is not possible for us."

"Have you consulted with the Elders?" Starlight asked, wondering what Gold's perspective on this had been.

Miracle shook his head. "Not yet. We have requested a meeting with them all. I needed to see you first, because you are about to visit a young boy, on Earth, called Mikey. And I'm afraid that I cannot let you do that."

Starlight frowned. "Why not? He is instrumental to

these changes."

"Not anymore he's not." Miracle waved to the clouds. "See for yourself."

Starlight turned back to the images, and sure enough, the young boy, who was once the fire Faerie Dictamnus, was nowhere to be seen.

CHAPTER TWO

"It worked? You convinced the Angel of Destiny?"

Mica nodded at his Flame. "She was a tough one, I could see she was suspicious, as she had already Seen the possible futures we have already lived."

Emerald nodded. "I bet. But she believed you were an Oracle? From the Thirteenth Dimension?"

Mica smiled and stretched out on the bed in their room at the Academy. "Yes, I believe so. When she saw that Linen was no longer part of the plan, I think she began to believe in my words."

Emerald lay down next to him and sighed. "Linen. He will never get to meet Aria. They will never run the Academy together." A tear escaped from her eye and slid down the side of her face. "Now that we are here, now that we are actually doing what Magenta asked of us, I am having doubts, my dear love."

Mica reached for her hand and squeezed it. "I know that fabricating these stories, and lying about our identity and purpose goes against the very grain of who you really are, it does with me too. But I believe Magenta. I believe in the vision she showed us. And that what she has told us to do will change everything."

"And bring us into the Diamond Age," Emerald said with a smile.

"Yes, about that," Mica said, propping himself up on one elbow and looking at her. "What the hell is the Diamond Age?"

Emerald chuckled. "I have no clue. I just knew that I couldn't say 'Golden Age' as I feared it might trigger a memory, and so I simply said the first thing that came to mind."

Mica shook his head. "You are truly amazing. It's perfect. It is the age that has come from much pressure and hard work, from a small black coal of an idea."

"And will hopefully be rock solid in its foundations," Emerald said. She stared into Mica's eyes. "I feel so conflicted. Part of me doubts our mission, and then part of me is coming up with yet more lies to make it work. Part of me feels such pain at the thought that we may be the only Twin Flames to ever be together, and yet another part of me is excited to see just how much the Earth Angels could accomplish if they weren't so fixated on meeting their Flames."

Mica sighed. "I feel the same way. I know what we are doing is incredible, and will change the world on a scale that has been previously impossible, but when I consider that we will not go to Earth, and not reunite the Flames at our Retreat in the woods... it makes me a little sad."

Emerald smiled up at her Flame. "I am so very glad that Magenta asked us though. Otherwise we might have forgotten each other too."

Mica shook his head. "That is not possible. I will never

forget you." He leaned down to kiss her slowly. "No matter what happens, we will always be together."

"Promise?" Emerald whispered, her eyes filling with tears again.

"Promise."

*　*　*

As all the tiny lights in front of him created an intricate, yet beautiful pattern, Tm felt his light dimming. Though beautiful to look at, the information they portrayed was not in the slightest bit beautiful. It was ugly, and it had the potential to damage everything that he held so dear. It threatened the very existence of his home planet.

When the lights finished their dance and dissipated into the sparkling air around him, he left the observation deck and moved back to his room. He couldn't face being around his fellow Zubenelgenubians in that moment, he needed to be alone.

Or, well, as alone as you could be in a planet of light beings who were intricately linked to one another.

"Tm."

Tm felt the whisper of the thought of his name through his being. If he had been human, he would have sighed. He turned to see Au, and acknowledged her presence.

"What have you discovered?" she asked him in the wordless way they communicated.

Tm only had to run the information from the lights through his being for her to understand with great clarity.

"Their darkness will spread this far through the Galaxy?"

"Yes." Tm could see Au's light dim and could feel her horror. It mingled with his own, making him feel uncomfortable. Their planet was one of light, where everyone was cared for, everyone had everything they needed. There was no suffering.

Yet, since they had begun to watch other planets, in the interest of preserving their home, darkness and suffering had begun to appear, and had infiltrated their existence like a disease. They had also sent Zubenelgenubians to Earth to help, but this too had left a darkness behind, where those bright souls were absent.

"Can we not just shut it out? Put up the strongest protections we have and just keep it away?" Au asked.

"We could, and we might continue to exist for many eons yet, in peace and harmony," Tm agreed. "But don't you think someone needs to step in?"

"We have tried before," she reminded him. "And our family have left here, full of hope to help those dark beings, and they have never returned, not one of them."

Tm knew that Au was specifically referring to Mg. She and Mg had been very close, and though they didn't have such things as relationships on their planet, they did tend to get closer to some than others.

Tm moved to Au and reached out his light to her, in the hopes of brightening her energy. "I still think we need to help," he communicated. "We may be able to protect ourselves, but what about the other planets they may adversely affect when they destroy theirs? It is our duty as beings of this Universe to assist in any way we can, for the sake of every sentient being."

Au moved away from him, and he could feel that she was hurt.

"I am staying. Go if you must. Save the Universe. I will be here, enjoying our light planet for as long as I can before the end."

Tm felt frustrated, an uncommon feeling in their world. "If we go, then it may never end, it may go on forever. As *you* may go on forever."

"Forever." Au was sad. "Forever without my loved ones."

She left his space, and he felt worn out. He recalled the lights and knew that no matter what Au thought, he had to go to the planet called Earth, and stop them from destroying it, and themselves. He couldn't live with himself if he didn't.

*   *   *

"Greetings, what may I do for you?" Magenta said, motioning for the soul to sit down.

"Magenta, I know this may come as a surprise, but," the soul sat down and looked the Old Soul in the eyes. "I am here because you told me to come and see you."

Magenta frowned. "I did?" she shook her head. "I don't recognise you, or remember doing so?"

"Which means it all worked perfectly. I have come here from the future. Well, from the second timeline, so I suppose you could say the second future, and well, I guess this is the third..."

Magenta raised an eyebrow. "Um, you may have to explain a little more. I genuinely have no idea what you are saying."

"Sorry, you didn't really tell me how to explain it to you. But you told me to do my best, because I need you to feed information to Velvet."

"Feed information? I am a Seer, not a puppet," Magenta said, feeling a little insulted.

"I know, but the visions you have had recently, of the demise of Earth, are now redundant. I mean, they did happen once, or rather, twice, but in the second one, you were on Earth, and you had a vision of the future as it could be, and you came home to the Angelic Realm, and asked myself, Emerald, and my Flame, Mica, to go back in time. But this time we were to go all the way back to the Academy to change things. Well, actually, to change everything."

Magenta knew her mouth was hanging wide open, but she couldn't quite close it. Emerald continued.

"The Earth Angels didn't wake up fast enough. They were too fixated on meeting their Flames, and they had not learned all they needed to thrive on Earth and follow their missions with confidence. You asked Mica and I to come to the Academy, pose as souls from a higher dimension, and teach the Earth Angel trainees what they needed to know to thrive, and also to ensure the Flames do not reunite. And for that to happen, it is imperative that Velvet does not remember Laguz. It is her remembrance of him, and her calling forth of him, that ensures all other Flames reunite also. If she doesn't remember, neither will they"

Magenta was stunned. She had not thought of the Flames since Atlantis, as they only reunited at the end of an age. She frowned "But, it *is* the end of an age. Why wouldn't the reunion of the Flames be a good thing?"

"Because it is *not* the end of an age – it is the beginning of a far grander age than anyone can currently imagine. But the reunion of the Flames would stop it from happening."

Magenta's mind was whirling. She glanced to the left of Emerald for a second, and saw a whirl of images, all seemingly backing up the Angel's words. When she looked back at Emerald, who was waiting for her to speak, she nodded. "I can See it. I can See what you speak of. And so I believe that somehow I did indeed send you on this mission.

I must admit, it has scrambled my mind somewhat. Does anyone else know? The truth?"

Emerald shook her head. "You told us very specifically not to tell anyone else if it was possible. We have fabricated a story, about being Oracles from the Thirteenth Dimension. We have worked out some of what we need to do, to ensure the changes, but we were assured by you that the rest would come to us as we needed it."

Magenta nodded. "I clearly trusted you, and from my new visions, I can See that I was right to do so. Now tell me, what exactly is it that I need to say to Velvet?"

CHAPTER THREE

"Another meeting? Right now? What is going on?" Gold muttered to himself as he called in an Angel to cover his position at the edge of the mists, while he attended yet another Elder meeting. It felt like he had only just been to one, and that one had lasted for what felt like an eternity. What else could possibly need discussing?

He arrived at the gates to the grand building where his fellow Elders resided, and they swung open soundlessly to admit him. He made his way down the path, the opulence of the gardens totally lost on him as he muttered to himself, consumed by his own thoughts.

"Gold, welcome," the Angel at the door greeted him, and ushered him in.

He nodded absentmindedly, and made his way to the conference room, where he found everyone already seated. He was the last to arrive, as usual. He went to take his seat, and realised that there were two extra seats around the table, with two unfamiliar souls sitting in them. This was certainly unusual, as the Elders never admitted outsiders into their meetings.

"Thank you for joining us, Gold," Silver said, only a hint of sarcasm in her voice. "We have called this meeting because we have two guests who have requested an audience. They are Miracle and Emergence, Oracles from the Thirteenth Dimension."

Gold frowned and looked at the two souls. They did appear to have a golden glow about them, but he himself had never even heard of the Thirteenth Dimension. "Thirteenth?" he said out loud. "I have never heard of that dimension? I thought there were only seven?" Despite everyone staring at him as though he was being rude, he could tell from some of their expressions that they had been wondering the same thing.

"The Thirteenth Dimension is an observational one, in that, we observe the Earth and other planets from there, but we do not interfere in any way. We have never even made contact with other dimensions." Emergence glanced at Miracle, who nodded. She looked back at Gold. "Until now."

"Until now?" Gold repeated. "You have come here to interfere in our affairs?"

"Gold," Silver said reproachfully. "Why don't we allow our guests to explain?"

Gold nodded, but couldn't erase the frown from his face, or indeed, stop his right eye from twitching uncontrollably.

"Thank you, Silver," Emergence said softly. She looked around the table at everyone in turn. "We have knowledge that, when taught to the Earth Angel trainees at the Academy, will ensure that the world Awakens and moves into a whole new era." She paused for a moment. "The Diamond Age."

There was a hushed silence, but Gold couldn't help

himself. "The Diamond Age? What is that? I have never heard of it."

Emergence smiled at him. "That's because it has never happened before. And without our knowledge, it would not be possible."

"Where did you get this knowledge?" Gold asked, pointedly ignoring the stares he was getting from Silver.

"From our observations of all the possible outcomes on Earth. We are able to See all dimensions, all possible futures, all simultaneously."

"So can Starlight, and she has been directing this dimension just fine. Why do we need you as well?"

"Gold!" Silver hissed.

"We can understand your concerns," Miracle said, speaking for the first time. "Rest assured, we are not here to take over. In fact, we have already visited Starlight, and she is working with us to create this new age."

Gold's eyes widened and his heart sped up a little. "You've seen her? How is she?"

Emergence smiled. "She is well. She was confused too, like yourself. But once she Saw for herself, she understood, and she said she would assist us in any way she could."

"Saw what?" Gold asked.

"The Diamond Age," Emergence said. She swept her arm towards the white wall, and it turned into a screen. In the space of a few seconds, the Elders watched the future of the world play out in high definition colour, and by the end of it, even Gold could come up with no reason why they shouldn't also assist the Oracles in their mission.

* * *

"I have called you all here for this meeting because we have two new members of staff, and they wish to speak with you about the classes they will be teaching, as well as some suggestions they have for your classes also." Velvet nodded to Emergence and Miracle. "It's over to you." She sat down, wondering if she should have introduced them, but their presence still made her feel a little nervous, so she had forgotten to.

"Thank you, Velvet," Emergence said, standing up from her seat, and looking at each of the professors sat in the circle. "And thank you all for allowing us to speak with you. I am Emergence, and this is Miracle. And we are Oracles from the Thirteenth Dimension."

There was a hushed murmur around the group. Velvet could tell from their faces that they'd never heard of it either. As Emergence explained their presence at the Academy to the professors, Velvet caught Corduroy's eye. He frowned slightly and she shook her head a little. He was undoubtedly wondering why she hadn't spoken with him about this before the meeting.

"We shall be teaching several classes to the Earth Angels ourselves," Emergence was saying when Velvet tuned back in to her words. "Which will include subjects such as Politics, Health and Nutrition, Harmonious Relationships, Entrepreneurship, Finances, Leadership," she paused for a breath and Tartan cut in.

"Politics? Finances? Are you serious?"

"Yes. We have foreseen that without a grounding in these subjects, the Earth Angels will be marginalised and unable to effect the global changes they are capable of. If Earth Angels understand the way the governments and political parties work on Earth now, and they get involved now, then the world will shift dramatically."

Velvet could see that Tartan didn't look convinced, but she was beginning to see the validity of the Oracle's statements.

"I know we would like to believe that we can send the Earth Angels to change the world so that these systems no longer rule," Velvet said. "But I can see that in order to change the system, you must first understand it, get involved in it, and then change it from within. They will not be able to change it from the outside."

Miracle smiled at Velvet. "Exactly. We have foreseen that if the Earth Angels remain ignorant of these matters, the world will not shift. It will descend into chaos."

"What do we need to change in our classes then?" Chiffon asked. "How can we ensure that the Earth Angels are fully prepared for this task?"

"There must be more focus on environmental issues," Emergence said. "The Merpeople must be trained in more depth on how they can get involved in laws and issues surrounding the oceans and rivers, and the Elementals must be trained in Earth-based issues. They are at the core of these changes. Because if they are too afraid to get involved, make a stand, and change things, the planet will be almost completely destroyed within the next eighty years."

There was a gasp, and Velvet felt her own heart restricting. "Eighty years?" she repeated.

"Yes," Miracle said. "By then, the oceans will be full of plastic and toxic nuclear waste. And most of the world's forests will have been mutilated and plundered. Not to mention that thousands of species will have become extinct, and the future of the human race will be in serious jeopardy."

Tears filled Velvet's eyes. She knew that the world was in danger of spiralling out of control. But hearing her gut feelings confirmed in this way was more shocking to her than she could have imagined.

"And you are certain that we can change this?" Cotton asked.

Emergence nodded. "Yes, we are. If we train the Earth Angels well, there is no reason why we cannot save the world, and its inhabitants, from this demise."

"In that case, let's get started," Suede said.

"We will meet with each of you individually, run through your lessons, and see where we can make improvements," Miracle said. "We have enough time to do this before the trainees for the next class arrive." He glanced at Velvet for confirmation.

"Yes, they won't be arriving for another month yet. We have time."

"Have faith, dear Old Souls, and Angel," Emergence said with a nod to Athena. "We shall create Earth anew."

* * *

The noise was deafening, and even with her tiny hands covering her ears, the little Faerie couldn't keep it out, it was really hurting her head.

"Larry!" she screamed, as she left her cosy bed and flew to the entrance of her home. "Larry! What's going on?!"

She flew outside. Her hands dropped and her mouth opened in shock. There was no green to be seen. Anywhere. The grass she had been tending to was gone. In its place there was just mud, brown sludgy mud, as far as the little Faerie could see. Suddenly, a huge monstrous yellow beast loomed towards her, the noise of its engine making her whimper in fear. She flew back into her home, but no longer felt safe. She grabbed her sturdiest leaf, and put some of her most treasured possessions in it, then tied a thread from her spider web bed around it, and tied it around her waist. Her heart was hammering the whole time, and she couldn't even hear herself think over the noise from the monster outside. She just knew that she needed to leave immediately. She flew slowly out of her home, and flew up through the branches of her tree, and then headed towards the woods that surrounded her patch of grass.

It felt like she had been flying for a very long time before the noise had receded and she finally felt safe enough to stop and rest. She suddenly remembered that she had left the rest of her berry stew in her home, and despite that being the least of her worries, she found herself bursting into tears.

She hadn't seen Larry, or Annie, or Lucinda. She hoped that they had managed to escape too. But her grass! Her beautiful patch of grass, that she had loved, nurtured, and helped to grow since it was merely seeds, was now gone.

Her sobs grew louder, and she wept for the destruction of such simple beauty. Though she had never encountered them personally, she knew there was only one culprit who could have wreaked such havoc and trained the monsters.

Humans.

She'd heard stories of their lack of respect for the planet, and for the Elemental Realm in particular. They turned trees into paper, and they turned patches of grass into nasty concrete hells.

But this was the first time she had experienced them in such terrifying proximity. She looked around her. She was feeling a little calmer but her tears were still flowing freely. She couldn't hear anything but the birds singing and the wind rustling in the trees, though she still had a faint ringing noise in her ears from the monsters.

She sighed, and wiped her tears with the hem of her dress. She couldn't just very well sit there crying all day. She needed to find another patch of grass. She was a grass growing Faerie after all, and she couldn't bear the thought of being out of work, not even for a day.

She flew to her feet and dusted herself off, and took flight to find a new place that she could call home.

* * *

Amethyst had never left the Angelic Realm before, but after hearing the souls from the Earth Angel Training Academy speak about how they needed volunteers to go to Earth, she knew that she couldn't spend the rest of her existence in the Angelic Realm, just watching Earth from afar.

"It sounds very scary," Larimar whispered to her.

She smiled. "It sounds like a challenge," she admitted. "But then even without all of the potential catastrophe, it would be a challenge. To be in a human body, to have human needs and desires, to not be connected to source? That's a lot to take on board."

Larimar frowned. "You don't sound scared though?"

Amethyst shook her head. "No, I plan to volunteer. I plan to sign up to go to the Academy."

"Really?" Larimar's bright blue eyes were wide. "That's so brave. I don't know if I could ever be that brave."

Amethyst squeezed the Angel's hand. "I'm sure that you could be, maybe one day in the future. But I know that the time for me is right now." She stood and joined the line of Angels who were signing up to attend the Academy. They would have a little time before they had to leave, and for that, Amethyst was glad. She intended to spend as much time as possible with her closest friends, and enjoying all the comforts and love of the Angelic Realm. Because despite the positive tone of the talk they had just listened to, she knew all too well that they wouldn't be recruiting Angels to go to Earth unless there was a very serious situation about to unfold.

Though she felt a little apprehensive about what she might be getting herself into, when she signed her name in gold ink on the ethereal scroll, she couldn't help but feel a little bit excited too.

After an eternity of whispering, hoping, wishing, longing to be heard, she could finally make the difference that she knew she was supposed to.

And she couldn't wait.

CHAPTER FOUR

Tm took his time to appreciate and absorb the beauty of his home planet before finally visiting Au to say one last goodbye.

"I still don't understand why you are doing this," she told him wordlessly. Her light was dim and her form smaller than usual, and it hurt Tm to see that. She had always been the brightest light in his life.

"I'm doing this because it *will* eventually affect our world, and I wouldn't be able to just do nothing and watch our home be destroyed."

"But to go to that wretched planet, to be stuck in a heavy body, how will you cope? Won't it just be too much?"

Tm merged his light with hers in the hope of reassuring her. "We are going to an Academy first, in the Fifth Dimension. It is a place for Earth Angels, where we will gain the knowledge and experience necessary to be human on Earth. I won't be going to Earth ill-equipped, I promise."

He could sense Au's acceptance of his plans, but her light remained dim, her energy low.

"I will miss you," he told her. "I will think of you often."

"No, you won't. You will forget me, you will forget your home, and I will never see you again." She held his attention for a moment, then moved away.

"Wait," he communicated. But she kept moving until her light was but a dot in the distance. Feeling heavier, and sad, yet still determined, he moved to where his kin were waiting for him, in the vessel that would take them across the light-years to the Earth Angel Training Academy, where his new future as a human awaited him.

"Is Au accepting?" Xe asked Tm when he boarded the light vessel.

Tm responded in a way that could only be translated as – "Sort of."

Xe didn't press him for further information and Tm was glad. He made his way to the navigation deck, where he had offered his services to the Galactic pilot, Jr, for the duration of the journey, and he resolved to let go of Au, and his home, and focus entirely on the task ahead.

He had the feeling it was going to be an interesting ride.

*　*　*

"I really think it should be you who speaks to him. I think he will listen to you."

Mica sighed. "Do you think so? He scares me, if I'm honest."

"But he was the one who told Velvet about Laguz, we need to make sure he keeps quiet. We also need him to remove the statue from the Atlantis Garden, it appears to be resistant to our magick."

"I know, I know." Mica kissed his Flame. "I will go and speak with him now and ensure that there is no chance he

~ 31 ~

will say anything. Although, now that Linen won't be here at the Academy, Velvet is unlikely to remember because there is no one to play their song to remind her."

"Let's just cover all possibilities. Otherwise this will all be for nothing. I imagine Corduroy will be in his classroom preparing right now, why don't you go over there?"

Mica smiled. "Yes, boss. Are you sure you're not from the Thirteenth Dimension? Because you sure are acting like a bossy know-it-all."

Emerald gave him a playful shove. "Oh, shut up. I'm just keen to make sure we do this properly."

"All the while hoping that they all remember anyway and it all goes horribly wrong." Mica shook his head. "You are quite the complicated Angel."

"Go," Emerald said, ushering him out the door.

"Okay, okay. I'm going." Mica stepped out of their room, which was in the wing that housed the professors, and made his way down the hallway, remembering to call in the ethereal glow that he and Emerald had been using to make themselves appear more highly evolved. He was still feeling a bit apprehensive about speaking to the Professor of Death, as he really was quite terrifying. But Mica knew it was important, so he did his best to step into his role as Oracle, and muster up some authority.

He reached the classroom bearing the gold sign stating – Death 666 – and he paused, took a deep breath, and knocked gently, half hoping there would be no reply.

But the door disappeared, and he stepped in to find Corduroy in the corner at his desk.

"Professor," he said in greeting.

Corduroy looked up and nodded. "Oracle. To what do I owe the pleasure? I thought our session was scheduled for tomorrow?"

Mica smiled. "It is. I just hoped to have a conversation with you now. About a very sensitive matter."

Corduroy raised an eyebrow, but Mica could see he was intrigued. He clicked his fingers and manifested a chair for Mica to sit opposite him. "Please, have a seat."

"Thank you." Mica sat down and called in every ounce of authority he could. He didn't pause too long before speaking, for fear of losing his nerve. "As well as bringing our knowledge here to teach the trainees, we have very specific knowledge that we need to share with particular people in order for the Diamond Age to be a possibility."

Corduroy frowned. "Am I one of those people?" he asked.

"Yes. We believe that you have memories of your life in Atlantis, which Velvet does not. We need you to keep those memories to yourself. We also need you to remove a certain statue from the Atlantis Garden."

Corduroy smiled. "Laguz? You're saying Velvet doesn't remember him, and you want to make sure I never mention him?"

"Yes, that's exactly what I'm saying."

Corduroy leaned back in his chair. "And why would Oracles from the Thirteenth Dimension want that? How does it affect the future? If Velvet remembers?"

Mica could see how happy Corduroy was that Velvet didn't remember her Flame, and it made him feel awful. He knew it was because Corduroy himself carried a torch for the Old Soul.

"If Velvet remembers Laguz, it will mean that everyone else will remember their Twin Flames too. If that were to happen, the Diamond Age will never be experienced."

"Why not? What's so bad about the Flames reuniting?"

"If people remember they have a Twin Flame, then they will spend the majority of their lives feeling like they are less than they could be, and that they need to find their Flame to feel whole. They will spend more time looking for or waiting for or missing their Flames than they will do following their mission, and living their purpose as an Earth Angel. Which would mean it will take them too long to change the world."

Corduroy nodded, looking a little less gleeful and a little more serious. "I guess that makes sense. It is an intense, all-encompassing thing, the Twin Flame union. I can see that it would be quite a big distraction from your mission." He paused for several moments before continuing. "So, yes, I will keep the information to myself and I will remove the statue promptly. Is there anything else?"

"Yes," Mica said, a thought suddenly occurring to him. "You must stay here. When Velvet announces she is going to Earth, and the other professors pledge to go with her, you must remain here at the Academy."

A deep frown marred Corduroy's face and he leaned forward. Mica resisted leaning back, in an attempt to appear unafraid of the professor.

"Why? With the fish out of the way I would finally have a chance to be with her. In human form. You have no idea how long I have waited for that."

"I do, actually, and I know that it will not work out. If you go to Earth you will have a miserable life. If you stay here, you can make a huge difference." Mica paused, wondering if he should hammer the final nail in.

"It wouldn't work out between us?" Corduroy asked, his gaze downcast.

Mica felt bad for the Professor of Death now. He looked bereft. "No, it wouldn't. It would be like Atlantis all over again."

When the professor's gaze snapped up to meet his, Mica knew that he had pierced him through the heart with his words. Even though he desperately wanted to apologise, Mica stayed silent.

Several minutes passed before Corduroy finally spoke. "So I just stay up here? What will I do?"

"It will all unfold as it is meant to. But be assured that you will have an important role here. Do you agree to do as I am asking?"

Corduroy nodded. "Yes. I'll keep quiet. I'll stay here. And I will remove the statue. But I want to be kept in the loop, okay? I hate not knowing what is going on."

"We will tell you all we can, when we can," Mica assured him in the vaguest way possible. The truth was, they were making it up as they went along, but he couldn't tell the professor that. He stood up and bowed his head slightly. "Thank you for your time, I will see you tomorrow to go over lesson plans."

Corduroy nodded and Mica left, noticing that the professor pulled out a photograph from the desk drawer as he turned away. He would have bet anything that it was a photo of Velvet.

*　*　*

No matter how many times she watched it, the images didn't change back to the way they were before the Oracles' arrival. Starlight was getting frustrated, which was a very human emotion that she was not accustomed to feeling. The new images didn't make sense to her. But that could be because she was resisting them so deeply. She was still feeling put out at being told how to run her own dimension. And she was still suspicious of the so-called Oracles. Who were they really?

Even though she had not visited him in quite some time, Starlight decided to pay Gold a visit. Miracle had said they were meeting with the Elders, and Starlight needed to know the outcome of the meeting. Because all of her original plans were shot now, and she just didn't know how to move forward.

With the simple thought of her love, she was instantly transported to his side, on the edge of the mists.

"Starlight!" he exclaimed, looking shocked.

She smiled. "Gold, my dear love. I am sorry to surprise you, but I am in need of counsel."

Gold reached out and hugged her, and she returned his embrace, breathing in his scent that she missed while she was at home in the stars. She released him, and stepped back a little.

"I need to know the outcome of the Elder meeting with the Oracles," she said, getting straight to the point.

Gold frowned. "They showed us the Diamond Age. We agreed to help them," he said simply.

"The Elders were not suspicious?" she asked.

"Suspicious? Of the Oracles?" Gold shook his head. "They weren't. But *I* was. I asked many more questions than the others. For I have never even heard of the Thirteenth Dimension."

"Me neither," Starlight said softly. "Do you really believe it exists? Or do you think there is more to their story that they are not revealing?"

Gold considered her words. "Quite possibly. I got the feeling they were hiding something. But at the same time, the future they showed us was compelling. Even if they aren't being completely transparent, if they really are able to guide the world towards that future, I think perhaps we should just do as they ask."

Starlight sighed. "I hear you. And perhaps whatever they are hiding is for the good of the world. That if we knew their secrets, we would steer things differently. But it's still..."

"Irritating? Annoying? Frustrating?" Gold filled in.

Starlight laughed. "Yes. Very much so. I had plans which are now moot. And I have no idea what I should be doing instead."

"You are the Angel of Destiny," Gold said, reaching out to touch her arm. "Just listen to yourself, and you will know what to do. Or request a meeting with the Oracles, and ask them to specify your path."

Starlight nodded. "You are right. I have just not tuned into myself since the changes have come about. I'm sure if I did, I would know what to do. I have been resisting because I am still holding onto the old possibilities."

"I understand, my love. I can be a stubborn old fool sometimes too."

Starlight laughed again, feeling a bit lighter. Her Flame always knew what to say to lift her energy. "Thank you," she said, leaning in to kiss him on the cheek. "I will see you again soon."

Gold's cheeks flushed a deep red and he nodded. "I look forward to it."

Starlight smiled and thought of her home in the stars, returning there in the blink of an eye.

She breathed in deeply, and closed her eyes, determined to go within and find her new path.

CHAPTER FIVE

"Why did you tell Corduroy he had to stay?"

Mica shook his head. "I'm not totally sure yet, but while speaking to him it occurred to me that if the Professor of Death was not on Earth, then perhaps there would be less war, and poverty and genocide. But I'm not sure why that would be. It's not as though Corduroy himself was responsible for any of that."

"But he was responsible for the fall of Atlantis," Emerald said, her eyes growing wide. "Which means that perhaps his energy would have affected the fate of the world." She kissed her Flame deeply. "Mica, you're a genius!"

Mica blushed. "Just doing what we've been doing so far, making it up on the spot and trusting the intuitions that come."

"Do you think there are other professors who should remain behind?" Emerald mused, running the different professors through her mind. "Now that Linen isn't coming, and the Children aren't coming, there will be no school, but there could be something else here?"

"Wait, the Children aren't coming?" Mica repeated.

"Why not?"

"Because there will be no one here to teach them. And we will be able to create the Diamond Age without their aid."

Mica shook his head. "No, the Children need to be there. Isn't that why we are creating this world? For them to have a beautiful place to experience human life?"

Emerald frowned. "We've never really discussed why we are creating this world. We just are. And the Children live on incredible planets that far surpass Earth in beauty. Why would they need to leave their homes?"

Mica frowned too. "I don't know. I just cannot imagine Earth being as amazing as Magenta's vision without them. Can we not at least give them the option?"

"I guess it wouldn't hurt. But we don't have to think about that for quite some time yet."

"Well, I guess not until the trainees arrive, and the second years."

"Not for many years, actually," Emerald corrected him.

"Years? But time is different here and the Earth Angels are here for a mere few weeks?"

"How could we possibly teach them everything we need to in just a few weeks? It would be impossible. I realised today, whilst sitting in the Angelic Garden, that we need to speak with the Elders and make sure that time remains the same here as on Earth. So that we have plenty of time to properly train the Earth Angels."

Mica nodded slowly. "Now that does make sense. Do you think it was the change in time that caused things to go wrong last time? That the Earth Angels were just not given enough training?"

Emerald shook her head. "No, because they still weren't

being taught what they really needed to thrive on Earth. Even if they had been here for many years they still would have been unprepared and they still would have been focused on their Flame and not their mission."

"Oh!" Mica exclaimed suddenly, making Emerald jump a little.

"What is it?" she asked.

"The second years. How will they come? Originally it was Linen's return to the Academy that started the wave of Earth Angels returning here. Without Linen, how will they be inspired to follow suit?"

"Oh," Emerald said. "I hadn't thought of that. Darn, you're right. There won't be a trigger to get Earth Angels to return." She sighed. "This changing everything thing is really quite difficult. You take one thread away and all the threads that were once tied to it disappear too."

Mica nodded. "In essence, you only have to change one thing to change everything. Just the fact that we are here, before the class even starts, is changing so much. But with all of our lies..." he shook his head. "It is already a very different picture to the original."

"I will think about how to get the second years here," Emerald said. "Let's not worry about that just yet. Let's just focus on the trainees for now. What are we going to tell the professors to do differently?"

*　*　*

The green Faerie was so tired that her wings drooped behind her as she sat on an oak tree branch.

"It's no good," she said to the robin resting beside her. "I just cannot find a new patch of grass. There are none that aren't already tended to or that haven't been destroyed." She sighed. "What shall I do?"

A tear slid down her cheek, and fell like a lone raindrop, to the ground, several feet below. The robin chirped and she frowned. "What do you mean?"

The robin chirped again, the Faerie's tears stopped, and her face brightened. "There is? Somewhere else? Huh. Where do I go to find out more?"

The robin bobbed its head, then flew away. Her wings shot up and she flew after it, trying to keep up with the creature.

When the robin came to a stop on a branch and nodded at the floor below them, the little Faerie stopped beside it and looked down, then gasped at the scene before her. There were hundreds of Faeries gathered, all listening to a few souls in front of them.

"Thank you!" she whispered to the robin, then flew down to join the other Faeries. They all appeared to be clutching tiny colourful bits of paper, and were whispering excitedly amongst themselves. She came to a stop towards the back, and had to strain to hear what was being said over the chatter.

"We are looking for Faeries who want to make a difference, and who want to stop the humans from destroying any more of the Elemental Realm. So if you are happy with what we have discussed so far, and you want to save your world, please do come and sign up for the Earth Angel Training Academy."

The Faerie's eyes grew wide. She could stop the grass from being destroyed? That sounded brilliant. She flew as close to the front of the crowd as she could, and waited impatiently to sign her name on the scroll to join the Academy. She didn't know how someone as small as her could possibly make a difference, but she knew that she had to try.

Once she was signed up, the green Faerie went to find the robin to thank them for bringing her here, but they had disappeared. She would have liked to have chatted to some of the Faeries gathered, but they all seemed to be in small groups, with no space for newcomers. So she found a small patch of grass with some toadstools in it, and lay on top of the smallest toadstool. Her stomach growled, and she remembered that she had eaten very little since her berry stew. She sat up and looked around, and spied some juicy berries on a nearby branch. She flew over and sniffed them. They seemed to be edible. She picked one, and nearly dropped to the floor with the weight of it. She beat her wings harder, to stay airborne, and she made her way slowly back to the toadstool. She sat down and picked bits off of the berry. It was quite ripe, and in no time at all, she was covered in purple juice. But at least her stomach had stopped its grumbling.

She flew off to find somewhere to wash, feeling sticky, and found a small natural pond. She settled on the edge and carefully cleaned her face, arms, and the spots on her dress. She caught sight of her reflection and frowned at her rather dishevelled appearance.

If she was to make friends at the Academy when she got there, a new dress was definitely in order. And she might even brush her hair, too.

*　*　*

"Why hello! To what do I owe this pleasure?"

Velvet smiled at her friend, and took the seat opposite her at the small round table in the incense-filled room. "You're the psychic, you tell me," she joked.

Magenta smiled. "Of course. Hmm, let's see." She looked over Velvet's left shoulder, and allowed her eyes to glaze over a bit. She couldn't See anything at all, but began to speak. "I See two souls, strangers to this dimension, coming here."

"Yes," Velvet said with a sigh. "They're already here."

"Oracles?" Magenta asked, even though she knew the answer. She frowned at Velvet. "They are Oracles, from another dimension. Why are they here?"

"To help us, so they say. They have Seen the possible futures of Earth, and there is one they believe will come about with the aid of their advanced knowledge. But, I don't know, it all feels so odd."

"Odd?" Magenta asked, trying to be as nonchalant as possible.

Velvet glanced around, though who she imagined might be listening, Magenta had no idea. "I feel like this has already happened before," she whispered. "That I have already taught this new class and yet somehow..."

"Somehow here we are," Magenta said, finishing her sentence with a smile. Her mind was spinning, what could she say? She needed to convey the information to Velvet that Emerald had asked her to, and fast. Her gaze shifted to the left again. "The feelings of déjà vu are simply confirmation that you are on the right path," she said softly. "Not that you have done this before. Follow the word of the Oracles, and the Diamond Age will come to pass."

Velvet gasped and Magenta refocussed on her.

"What is the Diamond Age?" Magenta asked.

"It is the new age that the Oracles have predicted will come about on Earth. So it is true then..." Velvet sat back in her chair, and sighed. "I must trust them?"

Magenta nodded. "Yes. You must. They have come to help. And isn't what they wish for Earth what we wish for Earth too?"

Velvet was silent for a moment. "Yes, it is," she said finally. "It just feels like something is... missing."

Magenta's heart jumped, and she wondered what she would do if Velvet were to remember about Twin Flames. "I'm sure it will all come to light in time," she said softly. "How are the preparations for the new class coming?"

Velvet smiled. "Very well. The Oracles are teaching a great number of classes themselves, and they have directed the professors on their own teachings."

"It sounds like it is all going in the right direction."

"I hope so. They have told me I will be going back to Earth. When this new class is called."

Magenta's eyebrows shot up in what she hoped was a suitable look of surprise. "You're going back? To Earth?"

Velvet nodded. "Apparently so. They said it was my destiny to lead the world into the Diamond Age." She shook her head. "I have no idea if I am up to the task."

"I believe in you," Magenta said, pleased to tell the truth for the first time during their conversation. She coughed, wishing she hadn't burned so much incense, it was getting a bit too much for her. But she knew she couldn't allow them to meet on the beach, where Velvet's energy was going to take them, because it might remind her of Laguz. Part of her couldn't believe that she was the one who had set this whole new path in motion. She wondered if she had met her Flame on Earth in the previous timeline. She made a mental note to ask Emerald the next time she saw her.

"What else do you See?" Velvet asked.

Magenta blinked and looked at her friend, unaware that

she had zoned out. "Oh, um, I Saw that you were right, there is something missing," she said, having no idea why she was saying it. "And you will find out soon what it is."

Velvet smiled. "Thank you. I had better go. I have so much to get organised before the trainees begin to arrive." She stood up, and Magenta followed suit. "See you soon."

Magenta nodded and watched her friend click her fingers and disappear. She slumped back into her seat and sighed. Lying was a lot more work and required much more energy than telling the truth. She hoped that it would all be worth it.

CHAPTER SIX

"It looks like there's something missing," Mica mused as he stared at the empty patch where the statue of Laguz once stood.

"Do you want me to ask Corduroy to replace it with something?" Emerald asked him from her place on the jewel-encrusted bench.

Mica glanced back at her. "Might be a good idea. Otherwise people might start trying to guess what used to be there, and it might get back to Velvet."

Emerald nodded. "I will ask him."

"Speaking of things that are missing."

Both Mica and Emerald jumped at the sound of Magenta's voice. She walked over to them from the archway at the entrance to the garden.

"Sorry to make you jump, but I wasn't sure if you had planned to visit me again, and I needed to speak with you." She glanced around. "Somewhere more private? I could hear your conversation from the next garden."

Mica looked at Emerald and she winced. His Flame stood up. "Of course, let's retire to our room. We have soundproofed it."

Magenta nodded and clicked her fingers, taking them all back there in a nanosecond. She sat down on the chair in the corner, and Mica and Emerald sat on the end of their bed.

"So what is it?" Emerald asked. "Have you spoken with Velvet?"

"Yes, I have. She is experiencing some déjà vu, but I feel I was able to change the meaning of the feelings for her. However, she said that it feels like there is something missing." Magenta sighed. "I know she means the Twin Flames. Even though we are taking away all possible triggers of her memory of Laguz, I have this feeling that she may remember him anyway, somehow, unless..."

Mica leaned forward. "Unless?" he prompted.

"Unless you replace it with something else. Another focus. Just like replacing the statue. Nature abhors a vacuum and all."

Mica looked at Emerald. "I guess we hadn't considered that we would need to replace the reunion of the Flames with something else. But it makes sense, I suppose. The Flames were a huge thing, and a huge reason for Velvet's return to earth. Yours too, actually."

"I can imagine that was the case. But actually, I don't plan to return this time."

"Oh," Mica said. "You wish not to return?"

Magenta shook her head. "If I am not to be with my Flame then I would rather stay here. I am sure that there could be a need for Seers to remain here. Are the two of you planning to go back?"

Emerald shook her head, and clutched Mica's hand. He sighed. "We cannot bear taking the risk of losing one another. So, no, we do not plan to return either."

"That will change things further. Us not being there." Magenta looked at Mica. "Was I happy? Before I returned here? With my Flame?"

"Yes, you were," Emerald said softly. "You were very much in love, and hated leaving him. But the pull to make this all happen was too strong."

Magenta frowned as though something had just occurred to her. "Where are they now?"

"Where are who now?" Mica asked, confused.

"Everyone from the second timeline who were on Earth when I returned. What happened to them when you came back in time?"

Mica shook his head. "I'm not sure I follow. Are you asking if that timeline has continued in some way in another parallel universe?"

"Yes, I guess I am."

Mica looked at Emerald who shrugged. "We have no idea. Hadn't even thought about it. I guess I thought that they would just cease to exist as they were, but perhaps they are still living their lives, in a different universe, in a different time."

"What year was it again? When I left?" Magenta asked.

"It was the mid-2020s," Emerald said. "I forget the exact year."

"It seems so far away in the future," Magenta mused. "Yet apparently I was there only a short while ago." She shook herself out of her thoughts and back to the present. "Anyway, I just wanted to warn you that I told Velvet she would discover the thing that was missing soon. So you might want to think of something, so that she doesn't remember the Flames."

"Thank you for the warning, and thank you for reminding us to only speak here in private in the future."

Magenta smiled at Mica. "You're welcome. I will visit again if needed."

"We would appreciate that," Emerald said.

Magenta nodded. "Until then." She clicked her fingers and disappeared.

Mica looked at Emerald. "So, what on Earth are we going to make up this time?"

*   *   *

It was the night before the new class of trainees was due to arrive, and Velvet was feeling incredibly anxious. She had finished making her rounds of the Academy, ensuring the professors were prepared, and that everything was in place ready for the influx the next day. She felt strange though. She had fully expected to have to rein Corduroy in a little, lecture him on not scaring the trainees too much, but he was remarkably sedate. Calm and gentle, even. It was unnerving.

She had spoken to Athena, her trusted friend and the only Angel professor. The Head of the Guardian Angels had reassured her that despite the Oracles' prophecy of the world coming to its demise in just eighty years, they would indeed be able to change things.

Velvet could always count on Athena to lift her spirits. They had worked together for many years and Athena had always supported her. But despite their closeness, Velvet hadn't been able to confide her feelings of déjà vu to her, as she just didn't know how to explain how utterly familiar everything seemed to her, yet how utterly unfamiliar it all was, at the same time.

Velvet leaned back in the purple velvet chair in her office

and closed her eyes. A soft, salty breeze danced across her face, and she inhaled deeply. A glimmer of sunlight glinting on the waves appeared in her mind's eye, but just then there was a knock at the door, and the glimmer faded away.

She opened her eyes. "Yes?" she called out.

The door disappeared to reveal the Oracle, Emergence. Velvet smiled and waved her in.

"I apologise for disturbing you so late, Velvet, I just wished to check that all was in place for the classes tomorrow?"

Velvet clicked her fingers and a chair appeared on the other side of her desk so that the Oracle could be seated.

Once settled, Emergence smiled. "You have done magnificently," she said. "Miracle and I are most impressed. And in fact we wish for you to begin teaching more classes yourself."

Velvet frowned. "But the trainee schedules are already full to the brim, there isn't time for extra classes."

"Not the trainees. We have heard that many Earth Angels are returning home, and we want you to offer them extra training here before returning to Earth once more. Miracle and I will, of course, teach some classes with them too. They would also be welcome to join the trainee classes."

Velvet leaned back in her chair, feeling a little overwhelmed. "Athena did mention that many Earth Angels were returning home at the moment," she said. "Will Gold agree to this? We don't usually recommend that souls return to Earth so quickly, as there may be confusion if they remember their previous incarnations. They usually go home to their own realms again or stay in the Angelic Realm awhile."

"We know it is not the usual path offered, but we feel it

is the right thing to do. The Earth Angels are only coming home because they feel overwhelmed and under-prepared. We think that offering them the chance to receive more training, and to return soon, will appeal to them. We will clear it with Gold. I just wanted to make sure that you were open to them coming here."

"It does seem to be a good idea, and I do trust you," Velvet looked the Oracle in the eyes, and saw nothing but love shining from them. "I'm just not sure what I could teach them? And how will they remember any more than they did previously?" She chuckled. "I also have no idea how the trainees will possibly keep up with all the many classes you plan to teach them, let alone how they will remember it all."

"It is possible," Emergence said softly. "I have faith that it is possible for them to remember."

Velvet nodded. "I can see that you do. Please do speak with Gold. I will speak with my staff on accommodating extra students, and I will think of a way to explain their presence to the trainees, as they will notice a large number of students who will not be in their original form."

Emergence smiled. "You are indeed magnificent, Velvet. If you remember nothing else when you return to Earth, please remember that."

Velvet blushed a little. "Thank you, Oracle, I appreciate your words."

The Oracle nodded, then stood up. Velvet stood up as well, and without knowing why, bowed her head slightly. Emergence turned and left her office, and Velvet slowly sank back into her chair.

It was going to be a very interesting class indeed.

* * *

"Mikey, could you go to the corner shop and get some milk? We haven't got enough to last until the milkman comes tomorrow."

Mikey looked up at his mother and nodded. He put his toy soldiers down, stood up, and made his way over to his mother. She got her purse out of her handbag and gave him some coins.

"That should be more than enough. You could get some sweets with the change if you want."

Mikey grinned up at her. "Thanks, Mum!"

She chuckled. "I'll see you in a little bit. Be careful on the road."

Mikey turned to the door, and frowned when he thought he heard a voice whisper - "Don't go out of the gate. Stay inside."

Mikey shrugged it off and kept moving towards the door. Once outside, he paused midstep as he heard the voice again.

"Go back inside. Don't leave the garden. It's not safe."

The voice sounded so concerned, so warm and lovely. Should he listen? When he didn't hear anything for a few moments, he carried on walking, and when he reached the gate, he heard his mother call out.

"Mikey! Could you get some bread too?"

He looked down at the money in his hand, and realised that if he bought bread as well, there would be no money for sweets. He turned and ran back to the house to get more money, completely unaware of the green car speeding by beyond the red gate.

* * *

"Velvet is different this time."

Mica frowned at his Flame. "What do you mean?"

Emerald slipped her robes off, and slid into the bed. Mica followed suit and joined her.

"She's calmer, more in control. She doesn't seem to be wandering blindly."

Mica chuckled. "That's because we're telling her everything she needs to know. And because Linen isn't here giving her the visions. There is no uncertainty."

Emerald rested back on her fluffy pillows and considered his words. "It's more than that. I think that there is a part of her that knows."

"Knows what?"

"Knows that she has done this before. Magenta mentioned she was having déjà vu. I think she may know, on a soul level, that she has already taught this class, already gone to Earth, and already fulfilled part of her mission. And this knowing is what makes her surer of herself."

"Maybe. But it's not like we can find out. If we were to even hint at anything now, this would all be for nothing. We cannot risk her remembering anything. Even though she may have a feeling that this has all transpired before, she does not know for certain." Mica kissed Emerald. "We must keep it that way."

Emerald returned his kiss. "I know. I will not say a word. It just... makes me a little happier. Knowing that she has some awareness, on some level. That her soul knows she was reunited with Laguz."

Mica nodded. "I understand. I feel better about it too." He lay down and pulled the covers up. "Still feels weird – going to bed. We never did this in the Angelic Realm. But actually," he yawned. "I do feel tired enough to close my eyes here.”

Emerald snuggled down next to him, and he put his arm around her, holding her close. “I know what you mean,” she said, her eyes closing. “It feels nice to be warm in bed with you again. Almost like we are back in the woods.”

“It does feel like the night before a big retreat,” Mica said. “Although tomorrow is the beginning of something far greater than anything we could have ever achieved on Earth.”

“Yes it is,” Emerald agreed, as she began to drift. “Far greater.”

CHAPTER SEVEN

The little Faerie was a jittery mess by the time she was ushered into the main hall at the Academy with all the other new trainees. She could see other Faeries there, but didn't know any of them, of course. She could also see people with tails swimming like fish, even though there was no water, and other souls with wings like birds. It was all very overwhelming and confusing, and so different to the Elemental Realm, that the little Faerie felt close to tears.

But then she saw a soul standing near the front of the stage who glowed with an unusual aura. She found herself flying towards the soul, drawn to her light. Before she could reach her, the soul climbed the steps up to the stage, and the little Faerie saw her join another glowing soul there, and a lady with long white hair, and flowing purple velvet robes. The green Faerie stayed near the front of the stage, gazing up at the three souls in awe. Their combined energy was mesmerising.

"Welcome, all! Welcome, Earth Angel trainees!" The ancient voice of the lady in purple filled the room. "I am so pleased to see so many beautiful beings here. I hope your journeys were safe and smooth, and that you have already begun to befriend beings from the other realms.”

The Faerie glanced around her at the other beings, and tried to smile at a swimming fishtailed soul, but she didn’t smile back. The Faerie looked back at the stage.

“My name is Purple Velvet. At the Academy I am known by my last name. I am an Old Soul, and I have been running the Earth Angel Training Academy for the last fifty earthly years. In that time I have seen many, many beings graduate and live very successful lives on Earth as Earth Angels.” She looked around the room at the different beings, and the green Faerie smiled.

“I am so pleased to welcome the biggest class that the Academy has ever seen. In fact, there are still some who have not yet arrived; they will be here in the next few days. The realms that are here though, are the Faeries,” a high-pitched cheer rose from those with butterfly and dragonfly wings, and the little green Faerie cheered too. “The Angels,” a beautiful angelic note rose from those with feathered wings. “The Merpeople,” a dolphin-like sound could be heard amongst the ones with fishtails. “And, of course, the Old Souls,” a low-pitched cheer scattered across the room.

“The ones who have yet to join us are the Starpeople. They are coming from several different distant galaxies, and we are pleased that such a high number will be joining us for this class.”

The Faerie glanced at the fishtailed being next to her, their hair flowing around their head in an invisible current. She had never met a Merperson before. The fish tailed soul caught her eye this time, and she smiled. The Faerie grinned back, pleased to have connected with someone. Then she looked back to Velvet, who was still talking.

"I would like to introduce you all to two of the professors who will teaching you. I will introduce the rest of the staff later today. This is Emergence," she said, motioning to the female. "And this is Miracle. They are Oracles from the Thirteenth Dimension, and they are here to teach you all very special classes that will help you to be even more successful on Earth in your missions as Earth Angels."

The Faerie's eyes were wide. Oracles? Thirteenth Dimension? She'd never heard of such things before, but it sounded very important.

The Oracles nodded at the trainees and smiled, and their glowing auras brightened a little. Velvet returned her attention to the trainees.

"Now then, I am sure that you are all very eager to settle into your rooms and become acclimatised. Aside from a few things, the Academy is very much like the buildings you will find on Earth. It is our intention to make sure you get used to the way things work there as quickly as possible. You will be sharing rooms, usually two or three beings to a room, and you will be mixed up to ensure that you become friends with beings from other realms. Please open your left palms and hold them up for a moment." A hundred hands went up in the air. Velvet clicked her fingers and a number appeared on each palm in purple glittery ink. A collective gasp of surprise went around the room.

"That is your room number. Please make your way to your rooms and fear not, as soon as you have memorised the number, it will disappear." She clicked her fingers again and the side and back walls of the hall disappeared, so that everyone could leave quickly without having to file out through the small doors.

The green Faerie squinted at her tiny palm, and read the

numbers silently.

"What number do you have?" the Merperson asked her.

The Faerie looked up at her. "Five five five," she said, holding out her palm.

"Oh, great!" the Merperson said, holding her hand out for the Faerie to see. "Me too!"

The Faerie grinned. "Well, roomie, shall we go find our new home?"

The Merperson giggled. "Yes, let's!"

*   *   *

When the Oracle appeared in the clouds next to her, Starlight felt a mixture of emotions bubble up. The overriding one was of relief. Not that she would let him know that, of course.

"Oracle," she said in greeting.

"Starlight. I apologise for appearing unannounced. Are you well?"

Despite her frustration at not knowing what she was meant to be doing, no matter how much she tried to listen to her inner knowing, Starlight smiled serenely. "Yes, I am thank you. Is all well at the Academy?"

"It is," Miracle replied. "The trainees have arrived, and the other Earth Angels will be arriving soon too. I believe Velvet will be explaining their presence later. It is all going according to plan."

"Oh, how wonderful," Starlight said. She could see the Oracle sensed her sarcasm and she regretted her tone.

"Are you sure you are well?" he asked. "You seem... frustrated?"

Starlight sighed. "Of course I am frustrated!" she replied, unable and unwilling to hide it any longer. "I have no idea what is going on! In my own dimension! I feel as though I am completely blind and all my plans have been ruined."

"Why did you not say? Or come to us? We will answer your questions and help you to work out your next course of action."

"Because I am the Angel of Destiny! I am not accustomed to needing to ask for anyone's help."

Miracle smiled. "Even the Angel of Destiny needs help occasionally. Besides, it is I who have come here to ask for your help in this moment."

Starlight frowned. "What is it you wish me to do?"

"Emergence and I have been discussing how we can make it so the trainees remember everything we teach them here, and do not lose this precious knowledge when they incarnate."

"Of course they will forget," Starlight said, not understanding where his train of thought was going. "All souls receive a clean slate."

"I know that. And I know that their souls will remember. But I also know that the chances of them regaining a full awareness of this knowledge is slim. But what if it was possible for them to remember it all? Clearly? As facts instead of vague recollections?"

"I'm listening. What is your idea?"

"It's just a theory, but I am hoping you will know how to manifest it," Miracle said.

"I will do my best."

*   *   *

Amethyst sat on the soft bed and smiled at the Faerie who entered the room. "Greetings, little one, are you in this room too?"

The Faerie, wearing a bright red dress nodded. "I think so. Room 409?"

"Yes, do come in. There are two beds still free."

The Faerie nodded and flew to the bed in the middle of the three. She landed lightly on the covers, and rested there, her wings drooping behind her.

"What is your name, little one?" Amethyst inquired.

"I have no name," the Faerie said. "But my friends called me Red sometimes."

Amethyst smiled. "May I also? Until you receive a proper name?"

The Faerie nodded. "Sure." She looked around the room, and her gaze rested on the noticeboard. She flew over to it to read the notice pinned there.

"What does it say?" Amethyst asked.

"That we may decorate the room as we wish," Red replied. "Simply by touching things and stating our desire."

Amethyst smiled. "That sounds like fun, would you like to try?"

Red shrugged. "I guess." She flew over to her bed, and touched it, murmuring something quietly.

Amethyst watched as the bed turned into a large, curved piece of bark, adorned with soft leaves, and a blanket of bird feathers resting on top. "Same as at home?" Amethyst asked softly, sensing the Faerie was feeling emotional.

"Yes," Red said, resting on the edge of the bark and stroking the feathers. "I am excited to be here, but I miss my home. This Academy is too white, too sterile and clean for me. I like the dirt, the trees, and the leaves."

"In that case, why don't we go to the Elemental Garden after the next meeting in the main hall?" Amethyst suggested. "I bet there will be plenty of trees and natural things there."

The Faerie's wings shot up and she grinned. "The Elemental Garden?"

"Yes, I saw the sign to it earlier."

"That would be wonderful," Red said shyly.

There was a short beeping noise coming from the noticeboard, and this time Amethyst got up to read the new notice that appeared. "We need to return to the main hall now," she said. "It's time to meet the professors and be split into groups."

Red nodded. "I'm ready."

"Me too," Amethyst agreed.

CHAPTER EIGHT

The little green Faerie was back in the main hall waiting to be assigned to a professor, and was hoping that her Mermaid roommate would be in the same group as her, so that she would know at least one person. The lady in purple introduced the professors to them, but the little Faerie was finding it hard to concentrate on her words. The only one who stood out was the Professor of Death, because he seemed a little bit scary. When the lady in purple (she really did need reminding what her name was) finally gave them glittery numbers on their palms, she held hers up to her Mermaid friend, who did the same, and they squealed in delight when they saw that their numbers matched.

The professors clicked their fingers and disappeared, reappearing around the hall with the number above them. The little green Faerie and the Mermaid made their way to the number five, below which stood the Professor of Cause and Effect, Suede.

"Everybody here?" the professor asked quietly, looking around the group huddled around him. He nodded to himself, then spoke again, so quietly the Faerie had to strain to hear him. "Come with me."

The group of Earth Angel trainees followed Suede from the main hall, down the white corridors to his room, where his full name and speciality was blazoned on a gold nameplate on the door.

The little green Faerie and the Mermaid entered, looking around the room in amazement. There were screens everywhere, showing people on Earth. The little Faerie stared at one of the screens where a young child was cowering under a table while the adult appeared to be yelling at them. She frowned, wondering why Suede would be watching these things.

The professor moved to the front of the room, where he clicked his fingers three times. First, the screens went blank, then chairs appeared around him in a circle, then a new screen appeared behind him, showing a schedule of what looked to the Faerie like a million different classes.

"Please, be seated," he said quietly. The members of the group each took a seat in the circle, though the Merpeople just hovered above their seats in their invisible currents.

"We shall be joined by more trainees soon, when the Starpeople arrive. But for now, we will introduce ourselves to each other, and we will create names where they are needed. To begin with, I would like to tell you the name of our group, and it is," he clicked his fingers again, and the screen behind him went green. "The Heart Chakra group."

While the Faerie was happy to be in a group that was her favourite colour, she was confused. What was a chakra? Before she could stop herself, her hand shot up in the air.

"Yes?" Suede asked.

"What's a 'chakra'?" she asked, blushing a little as her fellow trainees all stared at her.

"Excellent question. A chakra is an energy centre within the body. Of which there are seven main ones, which are each attached to a colour of the rainbow. The heart chakra is here," he said, pointing to the centre of his chest. "And is associated with the colour green. I shall be teaching you more about the chakras in our classes, and how you can use colour to clear them if they become blocked."

The Faerie's eyes were wide with awe. She had only been in the Academy for a few hours, and yet she had already learned so much.

"Now then, shall we go around the group and get to know each other?" Suede suggested softly, clicking his fingers and then settling into the green suede covered chair that appeared behind him.

A short while later, the Heart Chakra group emerged from the classroom, and headed for the Gardens to relax for the evening. The little green Faerie tried to listen to the chatter of her fellow trainees, but she was just too excited to concentrate. Because for the first time in her existence, she had a name.

*   *   *

"I really think this will work, but we need to wait until the Starpeople all arrive before we get Starlight here to do it."

"To be able to remember everything, their classes, their friends, their origins..." Emerald shook her head in wonder. "It would be amazing. They will all wake up so much faster, the Golden, I mean, the Diamond Age will surely happen then."

"They will still need to reconnect with themselves, and do inner work, but yes, I think it gives them a far higher chance of Awakening."

Emerald smiled at Mica, who was sat at the desk they had manifested for their room, making notes on their mission so far. They were having to liaise regularly to discuss what they had told people. It was difficult to keep track of all their lies. They couldn't risk talking in the gardens anymore, so they were confined to their room.

"So which classes do you want to do?" Mica asked. "I think we have enough knowledge to impart to create a few years' worth of lessons."

"I reckon we will think of more as we go along. I feel that we should teach more on female empowerment, so the shift towards equality will happen so much sooner. I mean, even by the 2020s they're still not there, which is quite mad really."

"True, it's not just teaching them things that have happened too slowly, it's teaching them things that hadn't even happened in our old timeline yet. But what about things that happened that the planet would be better without?"

Emerald sat on their bed and frowned. "Like what?"

"Like plastic? Polluting the oceans? What if it is never used in mass amounts in the way it was? What if alternatives are created quicker? What if we teach the Merpeople to get more involved in environmental awareness so that the oceans aren't full of plastic by the 2020s?"

Emerald nodded. "Goodness, yes, that's a brilliant idea. And, well, what about the Internet? And smartphones?"

Mica frowned. "What about them?"

"Don't you think the world would be a better place without them? If the Starpeople don't take that technology knowledge to Earth? Or if they do, maybe they could use it for other applications. Perhaps then people might actually talk to each other face to face, instead of through a screen. They might actually talk to their neighbours instead of people on the other side of the world."

"Wow," Mica said, turning to Emerald to give her his full attention. "That would be a massive change to the future. A world without people walking around glued to social media? A world where people actually talk to each other?"

"It's quite inconceivable isn't it?"

"It is. What about the positive aspects of the Internet though? The ability to find like-minded souls, the way people could make a living from their passions? It wasn't all bad."

"I know there is good in the Internet, but it doesn't need to be so readily accessible everywhere. No one needs that much information in their back pocket. It stops them from connecting with themselves, and nature, and the people right in front of them."

"So perhaps just no smartphones and tablets?" Mica mused.

"We can discuss the specifics with the Starpeople, I am sure they will know what to do."

Mica nodded. "What about the Golden Age Children though? If they do come to Earth? I remember them being particularly fond of the new technologies."

"So? They were hardly thriving on Earth because of the technology. Most of them had not even developed their imaginations. They were too busy watching videos and taking selfies."

Mica chuckled. "I do love a good selfie." He sighed. "This would be a huge thing to do. What might we suggest the Starpeople use their technology for instead?"

"How about for medical purposes? Or to ensure food is distributed properly? So that there is no poverty? Better recycling methods? Cleaner energy? They are so very intelligent, but all the digital age did was make a few people very rich, and the rest addicted to a screen. We need a new model if we wish to create a new world."

"I love your thinking. Okay, let's make a list of other things that would be good to change, and then speak to the right people. The quicker we get started the better."

Emerald was quiet for a while, deep in thought. "Do you think we might be taking it too far?" she asked. "Do you think we should talk to Magenta first?"

"Magenta doesn't remember what it was like in the future. So how would she know if we're doing the right thing?" Mica asked, turning his attention back to his notes.

Emerald sighed. "True. It just feels weird, playing God like this. I mean, do we really know what is best?"

Mica put down his pen, and joined his Flame on the edge of the bed. "Magenta wouldn't have entrusted us with this mission if she didn't think that we would make the right decisions. We have to trust that she knew what she was doing, and that she knew we would do the right things. If these ideas are flowing to us effortlessly right now, I think we have to believe that they are the right things to do."

Emerald nodded and rested her head on his shoulder. "I know you are right. It just feels like an overwhelming responsibility at times, and I have human doubts sometimes."

"I do too. But at this point, I don't see how we can fail, we have changed so much already."

"But we could create a world that's even worse than the one we left. Especially as the Flames are no longer reuniting.

What if Magenta was wrong about that?"

Mica was quiet for a moment while he thought about their time at the Retreat. "I think she is right. After all, even with all the successful reunions we witnessed, how many of those Flames stayed together, happy and living their life's purpose?" Mica could tell from Emerald's silence that she couldn't think of any.

"Greg and Violet weren't doing so badly in the end?" she asked.

"You mean after she finally seemed to forgive him for killing her and her unborn child in Atlantis?"

Emerald sighed. "You know that it wasn't really his fault. But, okay, okay. I will trust that we are doing the right thing. But I cannot promise that I won't have further doubts."

"Doubts kill dreams."

Emerald looked up at her Flame and smiled.

"Kill doubt, not dreams."

*　*　*

When Tm and his fellow Zubenelgenubians arrived on the stage at the Academy, he was amazed at the sea of odd-looking beings who stared up at him. He communicated with Bk, a Starperson from Zubenelgenubi who had taken on human form, and he watched and listened as Bk then translated his thoughts to the woman in purple who appeared to be in charge.

After being welcomed to the Academy, Bk assisted Tm and the others in finding their rooms. Tm arrived at his room to find his new roommates had already claimed their beds, so he took the last one.

"Do you think it knows what we're saying?" the weird

creature with a tail asked the tiny creature with wings.

"I don't know," the winged creature answered. "They didn't tell us how to communicate with them."

Tm listened to the exchange, understanding their words only by running them through his internal translation system. Without that, they would have just been random sounds, with no meaning at all.

He saw them motioning him towards the board on the wall, and he moved to it, and read the words. It seemed they could create whatever they wished in this dimension, just by touching things. He wondered if it would still work for him, considering he had no physical body. He moved back to his bed, merged his light with it, thought of what he wanted it to become, and much to his amazement, it worked. The bed turned into a planet, which looked much like his own.

He heard a squeal behind him, and saw the winged creature clapping her hands joyfully at his creation. Spurred on by her enthusiasm, he shot around the room, sending out his thoughts to the decor of the room, transforming it into the most glorious galaxy, swirling with colour.

His roommates looked about the room in awe, and Tm glowed brightly with pride. He then moved to his planet bed and got under the cover of stardust, feeling an unfamiliar and unexpected wave of what he assumed was tiredness wash over him.

The other two creatures followed suit, and Tm heard a soft voice.

"Goodnight, Mermaid, goodnight, Alien."

"Goodnight, Faerie."

CHAPTER NINE

"Starlight!"

The Angel of Destiny smiled. "Hello, Velvet, how are you?"

Velvet got up from where she sat at her desk and went to embrace her. "I am well! My goodness, I have not seen you in so long, what brings you to the Academy?"

Starlight sat in the chair that Velvet had conjured for her, and took a deep breath. "I have an idea. For your trainees. I am worried they will not remember enough of their studies here, or their origins, and so I feel I need to do something to ensure their memories survive."

Velvet leaned forward in her chair. There was a stirring within her and she felt that she was about to find the missing piece of the bigger picture.

"I wish to give each trainee a star." Starlight held out her palm and a bright, glowing star appeared. "The star will reside within them." She stood up and approached Velvet. She reached out and placed her hand on Velvet's chest, and Velvet felt a deep warmth within. She looked down to see her whole body glow brightly for a moment. She gasped.

Starlight smiled and sat back down. "It will record all that they learn here at the Academy. This star is connected to a star in the heavens, and when they leave here to be born into their human body, all of the information will be stored within their heavenly star."

Velvet's eyes widened. "That sounds amazing, but how do they access that information when they are on Earth?"

"All they need to do is connect to the star within them, and it will activate the connection to the star in the heavens and all the information stored there will be downloaded, for want of a better word. Then they will know, with certainty, who they are, where they are from, and why they are on Earth. Having access to that knowing will ensure their Awakening, and it will speed up the process of the world moving into the Diamond Age."

Velvet was surprised to hear Starlight also calling it that. How was it that everyone appeared to know about the Diamond Age except her? She nodded slowly, aware that Starlight was waiting patiently for a response.

"I think it's an incredible idea. And I agree that with all of that information, especially with everything that the Oracles have come to teach them, they will Awaken so much faster, and the world will shift so quickly." She touched her hand to her chest. "Will my star record everything now? Will I be able to remember everything?"

Starlight smiled. "Yes, you will. I was thinking that once all the students have arrived, I can come and do a ceremony with them, to gift them all with their own star."

"A ceremony sounds wonderful. I think that's perfect." Velvet turned to the wall and consulted her schedule. "The rest of the Starpeople will be here within the next few days. But they will be in their own forms for a while. Will this be a problem? Should we wait until they have their new human bodies before giving them the star?”

“No, it is not a problem. The star will remain with them even when they change form. I shall be back in seven days, and I will perform the ceremony then.”

Starlight stood up and Velvet followed her. “I must go, I have much to prepare.”

“I look forward to seeing you again soon, it has been too long. And thank you for my star.”

Starlight hugged her. “You’re welcome. I will see you soon.”

Without bothering to step through the door, Starlight simply disappeared, leaving Velvet standing in her empty office, her mind whirling like the swirl of stars the Angel of Destiny had left behind. She tried to comprehend all of the new possibilities that would come from the Earth Angel trainees retaining their memories, but it was too much to think about.

One thing was for sure, it was going to change everything.

*　*　*

“Velvet! I wasn’t expecting to see you again so soon!” Magenta motioned for her friend to take the seat next to her in the dingy bar.

“Some psychic you are, Magenta. Didn’t you see me coming?”

Magenta smiled, but saw her friend frown and then shake her head, and she wondered what thought had just crossed her mind.

Velvet sat down and looked around. “Why do you

spend so much time in these dark spaces when you have the whole dimension at your feet?"

Magenta followed her gaze. "I usually end up where people expect to find me," she said vaguely, wondering how to shift the focus.

"Oh. I don't think I would imagine you here…"

Before Velvet could think too much about it, Magenta tapped her on the knee. "What can I help you with? New class causing you trouble already?"

"Oh, no. Actually, everything is going really well. I just came to let you know that I found the missing thing."

Magenta's eyebrows shot up. "Oh? What was it?"

Velvet smiled. "I had a visit from Starlight earlier. She has devised a way for the Earth Angels to retain all their knowledge they learn at the Academy. She will be giving each of them a star, which will record everything. To access the information, all they need to do is go within and connect to themselves, and they will remember everything."

For no reason Magenta could think of, her eyes filled with tears. "That's beautiful," she whispered. She wondered if the two Angels had actually thought of the idea, not the Angel of Destiny, but she would have to wait to ask them herself.

"Yes, it is, and it is something that we've never tried before. I honestly believe it will change everything, because the reason Earth Angels keep coming home is because they don't remember who they are or why they are on Earth."

Magenta wiped her eyes with the sleeve of her robes and nodded. "Not being able to remember is hard," she agreed.

"I admit, the idea of going to Earth seems far less daunting now, if I know that there is a way I can remember everything. I see souls on Earth, stumbling around in their amnesic state, and it breaks my heart."

"Do you think it will be easy for them to go within? It sounds so simple, yet so many souls do not take time out for themselves."

Velvet sighed. "I don't know. Maybe if we repeatedly tell them that the answers are within, they will at least remember that when they get to Earth."

"Yes, that sounds like a good idea."

"Do you See anything?" Velvet asked. "Do you See exactly what we need to do to create the Diamond Age?"

Magenta let her gaze wander off to the left of Velvet, ready to pretend to See something that Emerald and Mica had already told her, but was surprised when a vision appeared. When it ended, she shifted her gaze back to Velvet's face, aware that her mouth was gaping open slightly.

"What is it?" Velvet asked, looking both worried and excited.

"The changes have already had an impact on the future. I just Saw you, in a very powerful position on Earth. You have remembered everything and you are changing the world."

Velvet's eyes filled with tears, and she smiled. "Really?"

Magenta nodded. "Really. The stars will work. The Earth Angels will remember. The world will Awaken."

Velvet's tears fell and Magenta reached out to pat her hand.

"Thank you, Magenta. Whatever will I do without you when I am on Earth?"

"I will always be with you, dear Old Soul," Magenta said with a smile. "And every time you think of me, I will be guiding you from here." She lifted her shot glass and Velvet did the same, clinking the glasses together. They both drank them in one swallow, and Magenta winced at the bitter taste.

"Pity it has no effect here," Velvet said with a laugh. There was a soft sound of wind chimes and Velvet sighed. "I'd better go." She set the glass down and stood up. "The next drink is on me," she joked.

"I'll hold you to that," Magenta replied. Her friend disappeared with a click and Magenta motioned to the barman to pour her another drink.

*   *   *

"So humans think that when they die, they no longer exist?"

The Professor of Death nodded at the Faerie. "Yes, that's right, um, Ava?"

"Aria," the little Faerie said proudly. "My name is Aria."

"Aria, of course, I do apologise, I can never remember names at the beginning of term. So, yes, humans believe that their earthly life is the only one they have, and that when their bodies stop working, they cease to exist."

"They don't understand about all the other dimensions?" Shelly asked.

"No, they think that they are alone in the Universe, and that they only get one life."

"Not all humans believe this though," an Angel called Sapphire said. "Some are aware of other dimensions and other lives."

Corduroy smiled. "You are right, of course. We are simply going through the most commonly held beliefs about death that those on Earth have."

"Right, sorry, carry on," Sapphire said.

Corduroy looked around the Earth Angel trainees, who

were sat in a neat circle in the brightly lit room. "Can you think of the effect this might have? Believing that you only have one life and that death means you cease to exist?"

Aria raised her hand.

"Yes, Aria?"

"Might it make them live more fully? Be more daring? Because they only have once chance to be human?"

Corduroy chuckled and the Faerie blushed. Had she said something terribly wrong?

"You would think that they would take that angle, but actually, they tend to go the opposite way. They become so fearful of death, of nonexistence, that they don't take any risks at all, and they do anything they can to prolong their lives, but they don't actually fully *live* their lives. Which means they might just make it to old age, but they won't have done the things their souls are longing for them to do, and often die with many regrets."

Aria frowned, her wings drooped. "That sounds terrible!" she said. "Why would they choose to be fearful?"

"Such a good question, little one, and I think-"

A knock at the door made the group look over to the classroom entrance, where the door was disappearing to allow the Head of the Academy to enter.

"Good morning, Heart Chakra group. Good morning, Corduroy."

Corduroy rose to his feet and greeted the Old Soul. "Velvet, please do join us, we were just discussing how humans choose fear and how they believe that they cease to exist after death."

"Sounds very interesting," Velvet said, glancing around the room and then looking at the trainees sat in a calm circle. "I must admit, I had expected something a little...

darker.”

Corduroy chuckled. “I have decided to change my teaching methods this term.”

Velvet nodded, still looking a bit suspicious. “It suits you.” She joined the circle. “Please do continue the discussion, I hope to get to know each of you a little better, so that I know how best to assist you in your missions.”

Corduroy sat down as well, and they picked up their discussion from where they’d left off.

Though it was interesting, Aria couldn’t help but wonder what Velvet had meant by the lessons being darker. She had a brief image flash in her mind of Corduroy wielding a long black object and laughing manically, but when she blinked it disappeared, and she blamed her overactive imagination for bringing her such a weird vision.

CHAPTER TEN

"When do the other Starpeople arrive?" Emerald asked Mica at the end of the first full day of classes. They were in their room again, updating their notes and plans, which had now taken over half a wall.

"In the next couple of days. Starlight will be here to do the ceremony after that, so once each trainee has received their star, we can start to speak with them in more detail about the changes they need to make. They're unlikely to remember anything much from these first few days."

Emerald sighed. "Why do I feel so impatient? We will be here for years, teaching them all they need to know, yet the idea of waiting a few days to be able to start properly just makes me feel anxious."

"Time doesn't really exist, so your impatience is redundant," Mica said, as he added a few notes to a particularly complicated diagram of their plans.

"It doesn't stop me from feeling that way," Emerald said, feeling a little annoyed with her Flame.

Mica heard her tone and turned to her to give his full attention. "I know, I'm sorry. I just meant that we need to release any useless feelings and thoughts, and really focus on our mission." He waved his hand at the wall. "If we want to make this all work, we have to set our own fears and worries aside, and concentrate. If we start contradicting ourselves or each other, if we slip up and say something we shouldn't, then the entire thing could crumble and fail."

Emerald straightened her shoulders and nodded. "I know. You're right. We do need to focus. And allowing human emotions to take over is what got the world into the mess it's in in the first place."

"I love you," Mica said with a smile.

Emerald grinned back. "I love you too. Now, what do we need to do next?"

Mica consulted their diagrams and thought for a moment. "I think we need to follow up with Gold on what's happening with the second years. He agreed to it, but I haven't seen any arrive yet. We need just as much time to train them as we do the first years, so it would be good if they arrived soon."

"Good point." Emerald thought back to the moment when she and Mica had arrived in the Academy as second year trainees. "It will be interesting to see who comes this time, do you think it will be the same Earth Angels as before?"

Mica stopped writing and turned to her, his eyes wide.

"What, what is it, my love?" Emerald asked.

"We won't be among them, will we?"

Emerald frowned. "I don't follow. What do you mean?"

"Our past selves. Will they be among the second years?"

"Our past selves?" Emerald said, her mind now whirring. "You think there are now two versions of us?"

"Couldn't there be? In every time-travelling sci-fi movie

I ever saw, there were always past and future selves, and they always said it was really bad for the two to cross paths. What if our past selves mention the Twin Flames? It could ruin everything!"

Emerald reached out to touch Mica's arm. "Calm, my love. Let me think for a moment." She sat on the bed and ran though the previous few weeks in her mind. She went back to the moment they stepped through the mists, having decided to go back in time. A moment later, they had opened their eyes, and found themselves in their home in the Angelic Realm, where they had been resting between human lives.

"We *became* our past selves," she said. "We didn't keep our future bodies, our consciousness slipped into our past bodies."

"So there is only one of us now?"

"Yes," Emerald said confidently. "There is. We won't bump into other versions, I am certain of it."

Mica nodded, relief etched on his face. "That's good. That would have put a serious spanner in the works."

Emerald laughed. "It would have. Although it would have been quite fun to meet the naïve versions of ourselves."

"Do you really think we were naïve?" Mica asked.

"We thought that reuniting the Flames would change the world for the better. That was pretty naïve don't you think?"

"I think it was hopeful. We believed that the Twin Flame love could change the world. How were we to know that it is knowledge, an inner knowing and self-love that will actually change the world?"

"I guess you're right. It is the default setting of an Angel to believe that love will heal all, solve all, and Awaken the world. But that's because we know what love really is. And it is not what humans tend to experience and believe to be love, or indeed what the Flames had on Earth."

"I think you may have hit on another class there," Mica said. "Love. What it is, and what it isn't. How to love yourself, how to love others in a healthy way."

"Perfect," Emerald said, making notes on her class schedule. "The time of painful, heart-wrenching, desperate and unrequited love is coming to an end. It's time that humans understood what it really means to love."

Mica wrapped his arms around his Flame. "I love you more with each passing moment. You may have doubts about our ability to create this new world, but I can see that you are shining in this task, and that you are truly stepping into your own magnificence."

Emerald kissed him. "And it's words like those that make me love you even more in every moment too," she whispered. "Shall we... rest?"

Mica smiled. "Yes. Let's rest."

*   *   *

"Sit down, Angel."

Amethyst eyed the tiny bench warily. "I am afraid I am too big, I will break it."

Holly chuckled. "It will hold you. Give it a try."

Amethyst slowly sat on the bench, which was constructed of woven twigs, and though it creaked a little under her weight, as her roommate had promised – it did indeed hold her weight. She smiled at the red Faerie. "It really didn't look strong enough."

"Neither do we Faeries," she said, flexing her tiny biceps.

"But we are very strong. We can carry five times our own weight, and work all day with no rest." She flew over to a toadstool and rested lightly on top of it. "We're tough creatures."

Amethyst smiled. "You are indeed. I promise not to underestimate you or your realm again."

"What was the Angelic Realm like?" Holly asked. "Was it beautiful? Full of trees and plants?"

"It is breath-taking. A paradise. There is a lake where we watch Earth, and guide the humans. There were gold and white buildings, where we socialised and worked. There were forests and caves and fields and pretty much anything you could imagine."

"You could create anything you wanted?" the Faerie asked. "Like in our bedrooms here?"

Amethyst nodded. "Yes, though much of it resembled Earth, because we watched it so much, our imaginations and inspiration came from there."

"My realm was beautiful until the humans destroyed it," Holly said. She looked around the garden. "Flowers in the spring, grass so high it blocked out the sun, and thousands of bugs. I loved it there."

"I am sorry you lost your home. But just think of how many other Faeries might not lose their homes because you were brave enough to come here, then go to Earth and change things."

Holly smiled. "That's true. I would love it if I saved even a small part of the Elemental Realm."

"You will make a huge difference, I just know it. You are a very wise and intelligent little Faerie."

Holly giggled. "Thank you, Angel. I am enjoying the classes so far, despite my dislike of what the humans have done to my realm, I am understanding a little more why they might act in such destructive ways."

"Why do you think that is?"

"All the fear they carry. What Professor Suede said about all the consequences they fear, all the rules they must follow, and what Professor Corduroy said about how they fear dying so much that it paralyses them into non-action or destruction. It made me feel sympathy for them. How can they possibly make good decisions with all that darkness within them?"

"That's a very good point, Holly. It must be very difficult indeed. I know from my time in the Angelic Realm that they do struggle a lot, and they try to make the right decisions, but most of them cannot hear our guidance, which would help them greatly."

Three Faeries flew past, and greeted them both with smiles. Amethyst smiled back and nodded her head. She heard them giggling and wondered if it was because she must have looked a little silly sat on such a tiny bench.

"I hope I can remember how I feel now, and show the humans compassion when I get to Earth, and not just be angry with them for ruining the Elemental Realm."

"I am sure you will remember. And you will find a way to educate them on the importance of the Elemental Realm and preserving it."

"Thank you, Angel."

They heard a chime on the breeze and Amethyst rose to her feet. "Time for our next class. We have Signs 101 with Professor Chiffon."

Holly lifted up off the toadstool. "Oooh I've been looking forward to this class. Perhaps I can make sure there will be a sign that will appear when I have forgotten my compassion for the humans."

Amethyst smiled at the Faerie. "I am sure that must be possible."

*   *   *

Tm watched the symbols and felt his light dimming. Au had sent a message to him saying that the lack of his presence and the presence of those who had left with him was causing her soul pain. That their world was a darker place because of it. He felt heavy as he remembered her disappointment in him. He communicated back, telling her about the classes he was attending, and the souls he had met with the weird wings and tails. He tried to keep his message light and hopeful, in the hope of lighting the darkness around her.

He wished then that Au had come with him. That they could have gone to Earth together. But he understood her resistance to living such a short human life. Who would choose the pain and darkness and struggle over an eternal life of light and joy?

Him, apparently.

He closed the communication, not wanting his lower vibration to be transmitted back to her. She was hurting enough as it was.

"Hey, Alien!"

Tm looked up at the door where his small green flying roommate had just entered. He glowed a little brighter in response and lifted his arm in greeting.

Aria grinned and did a loop of the room before settling on her bed. "I just spent ages in the Underwater Garden with Shelly! It's so much fun there! I never liked getting wet in the Elemental Realm, cos it could ruin my wings, but here it's like you're swimming but there's no water! It's so cool, you should really try it!"

She was talking so fast in such a high pitch that it was a struggle for Tm to translate quickly enough, but he got a sufficient idea of what she was saying. He was quite fond of the little green creature, even if she did call him 'alien' which he understood to be a slightly derogatory term for a Starperson. He could sense that she meant no harm in her terminology, and that it just meant she was fond of him too.

He had no idea how, but the energy of the little green creature had lifted his own, and he no longer felt as low as he did whilst communicating with his home planet. The lights in the room dimmed, and Tm knew it was time for what humans called sleep, but all he could do was to stay still in his planet bed and dim his light so that it didn't disturb his roommates.

He wondered what it would be like to really sleep, and what it would be like to be on Earth. At least it wouldn't be too long before he found out.

CHAPTER ELEVEN

It had been a very long seven days, but finally, Starlight was at the Academy again, ready to gift each Earth Angel trainee with a star. Velvet had warned her that there would be more Earth Angels arriving in the coming months, so she would have to return and do the ceremony again, but they both knew it was important to give the trainees their stars as soon as possible. Otherwise they would be learning things they would not remember on Earth.

Starlight stood on the stage alongside her sister, and looked out at the sea of faces. She felt a little quiver of nervousness, then shook it off, reminding herself that she was the Angel of Destiny, and speaking to a hundred souls could not possibly cause her to be nervous.

"My dear Earth Angels, I am so very excited and pleased to be able to introduce you to Starlight. She is the Angel of Destiny. She is here today because she has something very special to gift to each of you to assist you in your missions on Earth. Starlight, over to you." Velvet stepped back and waved her forward, and as her face filled the wall behind them, the crowd of Earth Angel trainees burst into applause.

Starlight blushed, and waved her hands to calm the crowd.

"Thank you, Earth Angels, thank you."

The room fell silent, and Starlight smiled. "In order to successfully complete your mission on Earth, and to Awaken the world, it is important that you remember who you are, and remember why you have gone to Earth. Without this information, you may get lost. You may get side-tracked. And so it has been decided, that for the first time in the history of the Universe, you will be given a way to remember. Not just a vague remembering, but a clear, concise, and perfect recall of everything you learn here at the Academy from this moment on."

There was a gasp among the trainees, and Starlight continued, knowing she had their rapt attention.

"You will each be given a star," Starlight said, holding out her hand, where a bright sphere appeared, its rays of light hitting some of the trainees. "This star will reside within you, here," she said, tapping her chest. "This star will record everything you learn here, and when you are called to Earth that information will be uploaded to a companion star in the heavens, which will keep it safe for you."

"How do we get to it if it's in the heavens?" a small green Faerie called out.

Starlight smiled. "All you need to do to create a link between the star within you and the star in the heavens is to go within."

"Go within? What does that mean?" the Faerie called out.

Starlight could see the little one was blushing from her heckling but was also too excited by this new development to care.

"Going within means really tuning into yourself, loving

yourself, and listening to your intuition. Once you create that connection with your heart, the information will stream through the link, and will reside within you as knowledge. As fact. Not simply as a hope or a belief."

"Wow," the Faerie said, her eyes huge. "That's awesome!"

Starlight chuckled and she heard her sister laughing quietly too. "Yes, it is. And I believe it will be the reason why the Diamond Age comes to pass."

There was an awed hush again, broken by Velvet who clapped her hands. "Let's get this started. We invite each group to come to the stage to receive your stars from Starlight. After you have received your star, you may return to your rooms or to the gardens, and are free to relax before this afternoon's classes. Shall we have the Root Chakra group to begin?"

A mixed group of Earth Angel trainees went up onto the stage, and formed a line in front of Starlight. She took a deep breath and closed her eyes for a moment to remember the short blessing she had prepared.

A Mermaid was the first to step forward. Starlight held out the hand that held the star, and she motioned for the Mermaid to come a little closer. Starlight placed her hand on the Mermaid's chest, and the star dissolved into her, making the Mermaid gasp. Her whole body glowed brightly for a moment, and the mermaid smiled and bowed her head.

"Earth Angel, to remember who you truly are, all you need to do is find the star within. It is here, where all the answers are. It is here, where your truth is held. You are a divine, glorious, shining spark of light, and when you go within, you will remember that."

The Mermaid lifted her head and smiled. "Thank you, Starlight. I promise to go within."

Starlight nodded, pleased that it had worked. The Mermaid left the stage and an Angel stepped forward. Starlight gifted her a star and repeated the blessing, and the Angel thanked her, tears of what Starlight hoped was joy, streaming down her cheeks.

A while later, Starlight was beginning to tire of repeating the blessing over and over, but she couldn't help but chuckle when the green Faerie in the Heart Chakra group approached her. She was so excited that she could barely hold still long enough for Starlight to place the star within her and to say her blessing.

The Faerie giggled when she glowed brightly, and then grinned at Starlight. "Thank you! I was so afraid of going to Earth and forgetting everything! Because I'm so forgetful, I can't even remember my room number!" She held up her palm for Starlight to see, which still had her room number on it in purple glitter. "But now I'm not afraid! Thank you!"

Without warning, the Faerie zoomed towards her and wrapped her tiny arms around Starlight's waist. Starlight patted the Faerie on the head. "Just remember to go within," she said gently.

"I will!"

Starlight chuckled as the Faerie zoomed off the stage.

By the time the final Earth Angel in the Crown Chakra group had received their star, Starlight was completely worn out.

"I must go now, Velvet," she whispered, her voice all but gone.

"Of course, let's meet up again soon. I shall let you know when the new Earth Angels arrive."

Starlight nodded, then left the stage and returned to her home in the stars, where she flopped onto a cloud and closed her eyes.

*   *   *

"Hello, Velvet."

The Old Soul looked up and smiled at the Oracle. She motioned to the space next to her on the jewel-encrusted bench she was sat upon in the Atlantis Garden. "Please, join me," she said.

Emergence smiled and sat next to her. Velvet was beginning to get used to her glowing presence, and no longer felt so nervous.

"I love this garden, although it seems as though Corduroy has been doing some redecorating." She motioned to the brand new statue that had appeared. It was of a Mermaid riding a dolphin. It was strange, but she had trouble remembering what had stood there previously.

"I think it's beautiful," Emergence said softly. "How are you doing? The Star Ceremony went well?"

Velvet smiled at the Oracle. "Yes, very well. The trainees are so excited about being able to remember everything. I do think it will shift things so much more quickly on Earth. Especially with all the many new subjects we are now teaching them. I have been sitting in on some of the classes too."

"We may be adding in a few more classes soon," Emergence said.

Velvet nodded. "That's good, now that the Earth Angels will remember everything, it makes sense to teach them as much as possible. What subjects did you have in mind?"

"Signs, Boundaries and Sex," Emergence said.

Velvet chuckled. "Sex?"

"Yes, we realised that Starpeople may never have experienced what humans call intercourse, and it might be helpful to teach them how to have a healthy and satisfying sexual relationship."

Velvet nodded. "I think that's a great point. I don't know why we never considered these topics before. What will the Signs class focus on?"

"One of the biggest issues facing Earth Angels is loneliness and isolation. We felt that if we taught them the different signs that the Angels send to show them they are not alone, that they are loved and cared for, it might help them to feel connected at all times."

"Signs like pennies and white feathers and shapes in the clouds?" Velvet asked, recalling a conversation she'd had with Athena long ago.

"Yes, and also number sequences, song lyrics and the like. There are many ways the Angels connect with humans every day, but most do not see the signs, or recognise them as such when they do see them."

Velvet smiled at the Oracle. "I do believe that will also be a very helpful class. I am actually beginning to look forward to my time on Earth, but I don't think I will be returning for a few years yet."

"No, you won't return for at least another thirty years."

Velvet sighed. "That seems like a very long time to wait."

Emergence chuckled. "Perhaps you should sit in on more of Cotton's classes."

Velvet laughed too. "Yes, perhaps. Patience was never a strength of mine." She breathed in deeply. Despite her newfound excitement for returning to Earth, she didn't really mind being at the Academy for another few decades. It truly was beautiful there. "What will the Diamond Age be like?"

Emergence didn't reply for a moment. When she spoke,

Velvet got shivers running down her spine.

"It will be an age of awareness. An age where every soul is treated with dignity and respect. Where everyone is loved and cared for." She paused. "Another one of the classes we are going to teach is what we feel will be the roots of this age. The class is on self-esteem."

Velvet frowned. "Self-esteem? Really? How is it that important?"

"Self-esteem issues are the reason why the world would descend into darkness and chaos within eighty years without our intervention. When people do not love, respect and care about themselves, they consequently do not love, respect and care about others or about their environment. This is what causes conflict, hatred and crime. And as it is passed down through the generations, it only gets worse each time. Eventually, we would end up with people who care so little for their own lives that they think nothing of taking the lives of others."

Velvet's eyes filled with tears. "Because they don't understand that they are a spark of divinity?"

"Yes. They forget who they truly are. And that they matter. This is why the star within is so very important, and will change everything. Because if enough souls remember with complete certainty who they are, and they remember the information we are teaching them, it will be enough to cause a ripple effect and *everyone* will remember who they truly are."

"That's beautiful," Velvet said, allowing her tears to fall. She smiled at the Oracle. "You know, I feel as though we might have met before. You feel so familiar to me."

Emergence smiled at the Old Soul. "It is because I *am* you. And you are me. We are all one, remember?"

Velvet shook her head. "No, that's not it. Your face, your smile... I *know* you. And for some reason, whenever you are near, I can smell chocolate cake. It's quite bizarre."

Emergence laughed. "Oh, that's just my perfume. Eau de Brownie."

The two of them laughed loudly, causing some nearby trainees to look their way.

"I should go, I am waiting to hear from Gold. He has information about when the new trainees will arrive, and we need to create accommodation for them. He said there are at least two hundred that wish to come! Isn't that amazing?"

"More than last time," Emergence agreed.

Velvet frowned. "Last time? We have not had Earth Angels return in this way for more training before."

"Oh, um, I know, I meant, well… never mind." Emergence stood up abruptly. "I should go too. Miracle is expecting me."

Velvet nodded, and the Oracle walked away quickly, leaving her to ponder the meaning of her odd comment. But her thoughts were interrupted only moments later when she heard wind chimes, a sign from Beryl, to let her know that Gold was ready to speak with her. Velvet replied, and after one last look at the dolphin statue, she clicked her fingers.

CHAPTER TWELVE

"Are you sure you are happy with this, Velvet?"

Velvet sat down behind her desk in her office and smiled at the Elder. "Of course, Gold, why wouldn't I be? If there are Earth Angels who wish to return here for more training and then help us on Earth with the Awakening, who am I to turn them away?"

"Oh. Well. I guess so." Gold sat down and shifted about a bit until he was comfortable. He could feel his right eye start to twitch, and he found it difficult to meet Velvet's gaze.

"Were you expecting resistance?" Velvet asked.

"Yes, actually, I was. Although why, I am not sure. You have never let me down before..."

"But?"

"But this feels odd." Gold knew he wasn't being particularly articulate, but his mind was a whirl of confusion.

Velvet leaned forward onto her desk, and frowned. "Odd? What do you mean?"

Gold shook his head, unsure if he should voice his thoughts. He didn't want to share his confusion if it only caused problems.

"Gold, you can tell me," Velvet coaxed. "What is bothering you?"

Gold sighed. "It just feels like this is all a bit... familiar?"

Velvet's eyes widened. "You mean like we have done this before? Déjà vu?"

Gold nodded and sighed in relief. "Yes. That's exactly it."

"I feel the same way," Velvet said. "I feel like we have done this before, and we have already gone to Earth... but I don't remember anything specific, or what happened. I just have this weird feeling that this is some kind of second take or something."

"Yes!" Gold said, a little too emphatically. "I think we have already done this. I think that someone has changed the timeline somehow."

Velvet was quiet for a while. "If that's the case though, don't you think it will have been changed for a good reason?"

Gold frowned. "I don't follow?"

"I mean, maybe we have done this already, maybe this is a second chance. But what if it's for the best? What if we get to do it all again and create a better outcome? What if the world actually ended before, and we have been given another chance to do it differently? Perhaps the Oracles are the ones who have given us this chance. And if that's the case, then maybe we should just go along with it all."

Gold sat back in his chair and sighed. "I hadn't really considered that. I was just lost in the confusion of the familiarity. But you are right. If we try to work out what is going on, we might ruin our chance at getting it right this time. But, what if it isn't for the best?"

Velvet smiled. "I think we need to trust the Oracles,

and trust that if this is a second chance, we will make the most of it. I know I would very much like to experience the Diamond Age."

Gold smiled back. "I would too. And as much as I have been suspicious of the Oracles, I genuinely cannot detect any kind of malice within them. Their hearts are pure."

"Yes, they are."

There was a sound of wind chimes, and Velvet looked up at the wall to see an appointment on her schedule. "I'm sorry, Gold, I must go. We are ready for the new trainees, please do send them when you wish."

"Of course," Gold said, standing up. "Let me know if there is anything else I can assist you with."

"I will."

Gold left Velvet's office and returned to his place at the edge of the mists. He smiled at the Angel who was covering him.

"Thank you, I appreciate your assistance."

"Another fifty Earth Angels have returned, I have told them about the new classes at the Academy, and they have all decided to return there. They are currently resting in the Angelic Realm with the others."

Gold nodded at the Angel. "Thank you, Opalite. I will go to brief them all in a while, and send them to the Academy."

Opalite nodded back, then flew in the direction of the gates to the Angelic Realm.

Gold turned to the mists to await his next visitor. He didn't have to wait too long.

*　*　*

He stared at the now very complicated charts and lists

adorning the walls of their bedroom, and despite feeling a tiny bit overwhelmed, Mica felt a growing sense of hope.

"Hello, my love."

Mica turned to see his Flame enter the room. He greeted her with a kiss. "Everything okay?" he asked, sensing she was feeling a bit flustered.

Emerald chuckled. "Yes, I slipped up a little, but I am hoping it won't be a problem."

Mica's eyebrows shot up. "Slipped up? How?" He listened as Emerald described her exchange with Velvet in the garden, and his panic subsided quickly. "Oh, I'm sure she will think nothing of it. I wouldn't worry."

"I hope so. It would be silly to have done all of this," she waved her hand at their plans. "And then to mess it up with a thoughtless comment."

"Velvet will soon be too busy to think about it. The new trainees are arriving tomorrow. Bk told me there are two hundred and fifty of them."

Emerald's eyes widened. "Oh, the number has gone up again! That's brilliant." She frowned. "Do we have enough teachers though?"

"I've been thinking about that. If we don't want the classes to get too big, we need to find some more teachers, and I think I have an idea."

"Oh?" Emerald sat on the end of their bed. "What's your idea?"

"We get the trainees to teach."

Emerald frowned. "But they don't know how to be human?"

"No, but I am sure they have valuable information about their own realms which they could teach. I mean, think about it, now that all the information will be stored so they can remember it, wouldn't it make sense for them to learn more about their fellow trainees and their origins? It would make it easier for them to recognise each other on Earth, and more easily connect and communicate with one another."

Emerald considered this for a moment. "I can see where you are coming from. The Academy focuses on teaching them human things, and eliminating the magickal side of them, but if we kept their magickal side…"

"Then it could come in quite useful. I was thinking of how the Mermaids are such powerful, feminine entities. They could teach their siren ways, and perhaps the respect for the divine feminine would return to Earth more quickly."

"And the Faeries could teach how to grow and nurture plants, how to communicate with animals and other creatures…"

Mica smiled at his Flame. "So what do you think? We could ask the trainees to volunteer. Ask them if they want to share their knowledge with the others."

"I think it's perfect. And it solves our issue of not having enough staff and not wanting large classes."

"That's settled then." Mica made notes on a sheet of paper stuck on the wall. "Shall I suggest it to Velvet tomorrow?"

"Yes, it's probably best if you speak with her. I forget who I am pretending to be when I'm with her. It feels like I am Esmeralda again, and we are chatting over a cup of tea at the Retreat."

"It is difficult to remember our roles here, and not just be ourselves," Mica agreed. He glanced over all of their notes. "But it will be worth it, of that I have no doubt now."

"I hope so."

"Hi, Faerie, what are you drawing?"

The little grey Faerie looked up from his notebook at Aria and smiled. "I was sketching a vision I just had." He lifted up the tiny notebook for Aria to see. She looked at the image, which was a very detailed drawing of Velvet standing behind a podium on a stage.

Aria frowned. "But I thought visions were meant to be of the future? That's already happened."

The grey Faerie smiled. "No it hasn't. This isn't Velvet in her current incarnation. This is her on Earth in about sixty years."

Aria's eyes bugged open. "Wow. Hey, you're Leon, aren't you? I've heard that you can See things. Did you really predict the weather in the Elemental Realm?"

Leon nodded. "Yes I did, it was quite useful." He stared down at his notebook. "Here, I just seem to get snippets of visions, of possibilities."

"Can you see my future?" Aria asked, curious about what might be waiting for her when she became human. "Am I important? Do I change the world? Do I save the grass? Do I like being human? Do I connect to my star within? Do I remember who I am?"

Leon chuckled at the stream of questions, and Aria blushed a little.

"Sorry. I just get impatient and want to know everything."

"It's okay, I understand." Leon shrugged. "But I only See what comes to me. I've never been able to direct my visions." His eyes glazed over a little and Aria frowned.

She wanted to bring him back to the present because his silence and odd stare were a little unnerving, but she also didn't want to interrupt a vision, if that was what was happening.

After a few minutes, Aria shifted about and nudged him a little by accident and he snapped back to the present.

"Oh, um, sorry. I was just…"

"Having a vision?" Aria asked, perhaps a little too eagerly.

Leon smiled. "Yes. Of a large number of souls heading this way right now. They will help us with the Awakening."

"Oooh, that sounds good! Thank you, Leon! It was nice to meet you." Aria flew up from the toadstool. "I should go and find Shelly, we were going to discuss our plans for when we get to Earth."

Leon smiled. "It was good to meet you too, Aria."

"Oh! You know who I am! I'm sorry, I didn't even introduce myself."

Leon chuckled. "I knew who you were, your reputation preceded you."

Aria blushed again, a deeper pink this time. "Okay!" She flew away before she could ask him what he had heard about her. She hoped it was only good things. She found Shelly in the Underwater Garden, blissfully floating on the invisible current.

"Aria! There you are. I was going to go to the evening activity. Did you want to come with me?"

"What is it?" Aria asked. She had read the list of options that morning, but she had forgotten them all already.

"I wanted to try something called Art. Have never heard of it before, but it looks like fun."

Aria shrugged. "Okay, why not?" She grinned. "Race you!" Before Shelly had a chance to respond, Aria shot off towards the Academy.

CHAPTER THIRTEEN

Velvet was very glad that everything was now being stored in the star within her. Because there was no way she would have remembered everything otherwise. It had been three months since the new class had begun, and in that time, so much had happened that Velvet felt slightly dizzy just thinking about it.

A large group of Earth Angels, recently departed from Earth, had returned to the Academy, trainees were teaching classes, Corduroy was being calm and gentle, Starlight was collaborating with the Oracles... It was a lot to take in.

One thing was for certain – it was time for the trainees to receive their human bodies. It wasn't fair that the Pyrydians and Zubenelgubians couldn't communicate with the others in an equal way, and it also wasn't fair that the Synapsians could read every thought as soon as you made contact with them.

Velvet looked at the complicated schedule in her mind and sighed. She would have to do some juggling to make time for the session to occur. It could sometimes take several hours for all of the trainees to be transformed, and she didn't want to rush the process. It was quite a huge step for many of them. Losing their wings and fins was quite traumatic for some.

She suddenly got an image in her mind of a small green Faerie screaming whilst a blonde Angel transformed into human form, and she frowned. Why was she still getting these bouts of déjà vu? They had been happening since the Oracles had arrived, and it was unnerving.

Velvet checked her schedule again and saw that she had some time before her own classes began, so she decided it was time to visit her friend.

"Velvet!"

With a click of her fingers, Velvet had arrived to find Magenta in a purple tent, in deep conversation with the Oracle, Emergence. She shook her head. "I'm so sorry, I didn't mean to disturb, should I come back?"

She saw Emergence glance at Magenta and then shake her head. "No need. I must go." The Oracle shimmered and then disappeared, and Magenta smiled at Velvet, but it didn't feel genuine.

"Everything okay?" Velvet asked, her mind whirring. She didn't even know that the Oracles knew of Magenta. Why would they be in communication?

"Of course. Emergence was just seeking counsel on when the first Earth Angels would be called to Earth. I have assured her it will not be for some time yet."

Velvet frowned. Perfectly acceptable answer... yet the Oracles had said they were able to See all the possible futures... so why would they need Magenta's help?

"What can I assist you with?" Magenta asked, waving at the now empty chair opposite her. Velvet sat, and tried to organise her thoughts and remember why she had come.

"Oh, yes, I came to ask you again. Have we done this before?"

Magenta's eyes widened and her mouth fell open, which was all Velvet needed to confirm that her suspicions were true.

"So we have," Velvet said. "I have already taught this class? Already been to Earth? I have been having the strongest, most vivid déjà vu and despite your explanation of it being signs I'm on the right path, the visions just feel too real to simply be signs."

Magenta took a little while to answer, and when she did, Velvet could tell she was still not being entirely truthful. "Yes, we have done this before, but we have been given the chance to do it again… because the first time didn't quite work out."

"What happened?"

"Honestly? I don't know. I don't remember. But the Oracles have assured me that this time things will be much better, and the world will not decline in the same fashion, and that the Earth Angels will succeed in their missions."

Velvet frowned. "Why couldn't we have retained our memories? It might have helped us?"

Magenta shook her head. "The Oracles said it would have just been a distraction. That we would have been consumed by memories and unable to start afresh."

Velvet sighed. "I don't know if I agree, but I must admit that this new class is going well. And with the star within, I can't see how the Earth Angels could possibly fail…" A thought occurred to her. "There was no star within before, was there?"

Magenta shook her head. "No. There wasn't. And the Earth Angels did not Awaken until it was too late."

Velvet nodded. "I can feel the truth in that. Gold also suspects that we have done this before. Should I tell him?"

Magenta shook her head. "I believe that the fewer people who know about this, the better. It would just cause too much confusion."

Velvet sighed, and heard the distant sound of wind chimes. "Very well. I trust your judgment. I must go. Thank you for your honesty. I will do my best not to allow the déjà vu to bother me."

"I love you, Velvet." Magenta stood up and held her arms out. Velvet smiled and embraced her old friend, surprised but also moved by the display of emotion.

"I love you too, Magenta."

"It will work out for the highest good of all the Earth Angels and the humans," Magenta said, releasing her.

"I do hope so," Velvet said. "I will see you again soon."

"Soon," Magenta echoed as Velvet clicked her fingers to return to her office.

Despite not having long before her next class, Velvet sat down heavily in her chair, and sighed. She wanted to know what had happened in the first timeline, and why it had not worked out, but she could tell that she would not get any answers from Magenta, and it seemed pointless to ask the Oracles. If they had wanted her to know, they would have told her already. It seemed like she would have to follow her own advice to Gold, and to let go of needing to know, trusting the Oracles and doing her best to follow their direction.

She hoped it was good advice.

* * *

If it was possible for him to feel nervous, then Tm would have been shaking while he waited to receive his human body. To be confined and constricted into flesh and bone sounded painful and heavy, and he knew that he would miss the ease and fluidity of his movements. But he was looking forward to being able to converse with his fellow trainees, and being able to ask questions in classes. He often had so many questions but no way of communicating them, unless Bk was nearby. He had a lot of questions for Professor Indigo in particular. In their last Emotions class, he had been telling them all about depression, and Tm couldn't quite understand how a human could feel so isolated and alone. He looked forward to getting answers.

He pulled himself out of his thoughts and watched the other Earth Angels lose their wings and fins and he could feel the anticipation building up within him. What would it feel like? To be human? To walk and to run?

He didn't have to wait too long, as soon it was his turn to step up and choose the characteristics he wished to have. When his choices were assembled into a human form, he looked at it briefly and then took a deep breath, and closed his eyes.

When he opened them, it was through the blue eyes he had chosen just moments before. He looked around at his friends, and the Faerie, Aria, grinned back at him from her own brand new body. "Tim! How does it feel?"

Tm opened his mouth and found it was very dry. "Odd," he said. His own voice made him jump a little and Aria giggled. "I sound weird."

"You sound just like I thought you would!" Aria said. She stepped forward and hugged him, and the feeling of her arms wrapped around him was so comforting that Tm felt a strange liquid gather in his eyes.

Aria leaned back and looked up at him, her small form still somehow dwarfed by his, even in human form. "Oh, Tim, don't cry. We can still race each other."

Tm chuckled then, and nodded. "Yes we can." He moved his legs and was shocked by the weight. "Might have to get used to this body first though. It feels so heavy!"

"You will get used to it," Velvet assured him. "All trainees feel heavy for the first week or so. But then it gets easier."

Tm nodded at the Old Soul. "Thank you. I'm sure I will acclimatise. It's just a bit of a shock."

Once the Heart Chakra group had all been transformed, they left the main hall, and Tm found himself walking slowly towards the Planetary Garden. He found a quiet space in the stars, and turned his attention within, to connect with Au on Zubenelgenubi.

But there was nothing there. Tm frowned and concentrated harder, but the link that existed between them was gone. A ripple of panic went through him and he jumped up, and ran back to the Academy, feeling irritation at his heavy body slowing him down. He went to the wing where the offices were and found the marketing office. He raised a fist to hammer on the door but it disappeared before he made contact and his fist nearly connected with Bk's nose.

"Whoa! Can I help you?"

"It's me, Tm, and I hope so. It's gone. My connection to home. I can't find it."

"Oh," Bk said. "Weren't you warned? That happens once you enter your human body."

"So I cannot contact them?" Tm heard his voice raise in pitch but couldn't stop it. "How were you able to talk to us when we first arrived? When you were in human form?"

"I have had a great many years of practice, and I can still only communicate with those who are in the same room as me."

Tm's face fell. "Oh."

"You can still contact home, but not in the same way as before. You will need to come here, and send a light message."

Tm sighed, partially with relief and partially with frustration. "But light messages are not instant. They would take a great deal of time to reach my home."

Bk put his hand on Tm's shoulder. "I'm sorry. You were close to her, weren't you?"

Tm felt the liquid gather in his eyes again, and he then felt it trickle down his cheeks. He nodded. "Yes." In that moment a deep pang of loneliness hit him, and he begun to understand what Indigo had been talking about.

"Come in now and send a message. I will let you know when we receive a reply."

Tm nodded and followed him into the room, where he sat at a screen and slowly created a light message that would be sent through the Universe to Au.

Even if he never received the reply, he had to let her know that he would never forget her.

Never.

*   *   *

"Do you think things will be easier now?"

Mica looked at Emerald from where he stood next to their wall of notes. "Now that they are all in human form? I think so. At least the Starpeople can join in fully. And the longer they have their human bodies before they go to

Earth, the less of a shock it will be for them. So yes, I hope it will be easier for them. It will be odd though, not seeing them flying and swimming around."

Emerald nodded. "Yes, it was quite magical before. Now it will just feel like we are on Earth."

"Which is kind of the point?"

Emerald chuckled. "True. The trainees are really doing well so far though. I mean, we are teaching them a lot of information, so much of which is completely alien to them, yet they are taking it all in and understanding it. I'm quite amazed."

"I think they were underestimated last time. I think Earth Angels have an amazing capacity to expand and grow, and they need to be pushed beyond their boundaries in order to really Awaken those on Earth."

"I think you are right. They are infinite beings, not just Faeries or Mermaids or Starpeople. They are capable of so much more than we could dream of."

"Indeed. As are we."

Emerald frowned. "We are?"

Mica joined Emerald on the edge of the bed. "I have been thinking. I think we need to go too. To Earth. Not now, but when the last Earth Angels have been called. I think we should go with Velvet."

Emerald's eyes widened and she gasped. "But… what if we forget each other? What if we do not find each other?"

"I have already thought of that." Mica reached into his pocket and pulled out two stars. They lit up the bedroom, and Emerald blinked. "If we have stars, all we need to do is go within, and we will remember all of this. And we will remember each other."

Emerald felt the tears on her cheeks before she was

aware she was crying. "Are you sure? Will we really find each other? The Flames aren't meant to reunite. What if our reunion ruins everything?"

Mica chuckled. "I somehow don't think we have the power to ruin everything we have set in motion. It's too big for that now. And yes, I am sure I will find you. Or you will find me. So what do you say? It won't be for many years yet, but if we are going, then we need to place these within now." He held a star out to her, and Emerald breathed in deeply before taking it from him and nodding.

"Okay, I trust you," she whispered. She pressed the star into the centre of her chest and she felt it sink into the core of her being, making her whole body glow for a moment. Mica did the same, and Emerald smiled as his body glowed brightly too, making him seem even more angelic than normal.

"It will be an adventure, and besides, don't you want to experience this magical Diamond Age we are creating?"

Emerald sighed. "I guess so. I just cannot bear the thought of not being with you, even for a short while."

Mica pulled her into his arms and held her tight. "I know. I don't relish the thought either, but I feel it will be important for us to witness it in person. Not just from here. And I trust that it will all work out as it should."

Emerald breathed in his scent deeply and closed her eyes. "I love you, Mica."

"As I love you, Emerald. Always."

CHAPTER FOURTEEN

"Oh! I'm so sorry!" Amethyst stepped away from the soul she had just walked into, and blinked.

"Don't worry, no harm done," the soul in bright blue robes replied. "Are you okay?"

Amethyst nodded, and frowned. "Do I know you?"

The soul shook their head. "I don't think so. I would remember you, I am sure."

Amethyst blushed. "My name is Amethyst."

"Cobalt," he replied, holding his hand out.

Amethyst looked at his hand, unsure what to do.

"On Earth, when you meet people you shake hands."

"Oh, yes, I remember seeing them do that, but I never understood why?" Amethyst said, reaching out to grasp his hand and shake it.

Cobalt laughed. "I have no idea. It's their more formal greeting. I never questioned it, to be honest. Humans are odd creatures."

Amethyst had half expected a bolt of lightning to hit her when their hands touched, but there was nothing. She looked into his eyes and saw no recognition there. She decided she was just tired and imagining things.

"I apologise again for walking right into you. I will look where I am going next time."

Cobalt chuckled. "Sounds like a good idea. I should go, I have a class. Have a wonderful day."

Amethyst nodded, and murmured. "You too." She watched him walk away, and felt a weird ache in her chest. *This human body is going to take a while to get used to,* she thought to herself.

"Amethyst! Are you coming?"

Amethyst turned to see Holly beckoning her from the entrance to the Elemental Garden and she nodded, trying to shake off all the weird feelings.

*   *   *

"You called, my love?"

Gold saw Starlight emerging from the mists and he smiled. "Yes, I did. I wished to know the current state of affairs."

Starlight frowned. "In what way?"

"The changes in this dimension over the last few months have been unprecedented, and I was hoping for an update on whether we were still on course for this promised Diamond Age?"

"Oh. I must admit I have not checked recently. Let's have a look shall we?"

Starlight waved her hand and the mists swirled up and images began appearing, flickering and whirling, taking Starlight and Gold on a journey from the present moment on Earth through the next hundred years.

When the last image faded away, Gold blinked and

looked at the Angel of Destiny. He was glad to see that she too, was crying tears of joy.

"I have never seen... it was so..."

He smiled as she struggled to find the words to describe what they had just witnessed.

"It will be a heaven on Earth."

Starlight nodded and wiped her tears away with her sleeve. "It will. How incredible is that? I had my doubts when the Oracles appeared from nowhere, professing to know so much about the future, but it would appear that they were right after all."

Gold nodded. "I had my reservations, and I'm still not sure if I believe they are from the Thirteenth Dimension, but it would seem that their intervention will create the world we have been trying to create for some time."

"It looks that way." Starlight reached out to touch his arm. "Perhaps when the Diamond Age happens you will finally join me?"

"In the stars?"

"Yes. It has been so long."

Gold sighed. "Too long. But my work here..."

"I know. It is important, but, well, please consider it."

"I will, I promise. When the time is right, I will come home to you."

Starlight smiled. "Good. I look forward to that moment. But for now I must go. More Earth Angels have arrived at the Academy and they are ready to receive their stars."

"It was a wonderful idea, giving them a star within so they would remember everything. However did you think of it?" Gold asked curiously.

Starlight grinned. "The Angel of Destiny never reveals her secrets," she said mysteriously.

Gold chuckled. "I understand. But promise you will reveal them one day?"

Starlight nodded. "I promise. One day, I will tell you everything."

"When I return to the stars?"

"Yes," Starlight said, as she began to disappear. "When you come home to me."

"Home," Gold said to the swirl of lights she left behind. "I cannot wait."

*   *   *

"It's really not so bad, being human. The body is a bit weird, and not having wings really does suck, but all the awesome things they get to do? So cool! I think art and music are my favourite activities, and Human Culture is my favourite class. What about you?"

Rosa smiled at Aria as they walked down the white hallways of the Academy. "I think my favourite class is politics, actually."

Aria wrinkled her nose. "Really? It seems a bit boring to me."

"But it's so important! If we really want to make a difference, to see the Diamond Age, we need to know how to change things from within the existing systems."

"You sound like Miracle," Aria commented. "Don't forget that Faeries are supposed to bring fun to the planet."

Rosa giggled. "I think you can be involved in politics and still have fun. The two aren't mutually exclusive."

Aria shrugged. "I guess. I suppose I just don't fully understand it. Would you explain it to me? In terms I would understand?"

Rosa smiled. "Of course, I would love to. Do you think there are others who feel the same? Perhaps we should create a little study group?"

"Oh, that sounds fun! Although when we would have time to do it? Our schedule is nuts isn't it?"

"It is. I thought we would have a bit more time to relax."

They reached their next class, Harmonic Relationships with Emergence, and they entered the classroom. Their classmates were already there, along with a group of second years.

"Welcome, Earth Angels, please do make yourself comfortable. Today, we are going to discuss what it is to have respect for your partner, as well as respect for yourself."

Aria and Rosa found a couple of chairs next to each other, and sat down. Although Aria found the idea of having a relationship with another soul a weird concept, she had to admit, she was also kind of looking forward to that aspect of her earthly life. She shook herself out of her thoughts and focused her full attention on the Oracle in front of her, determined not to miss a thing.

When she and Rosa emerged an hour later, Aria's mind was whirling. "Wow. Do you really think it's possible? To have the kind of relationship that Emergence was describing?"

Rosa shrugged. "I don't see why not. We respect our fellow Faeries in the Elemental Realm, regardless of their differing beliefs, so it should be possible between humans?"

"But how can humans respect each other when they clearly have no respect for their planet? They are ruining their own home. That's not very respectful at all."

"True," Rosa said with a sigh. They walked in silence towards their next class, which was Politics with Miracle.

"Hopefully it will improve once all the Earth Angels are there with all this new knowledge."

Aria smiled at Rosa. "I'm sure you're right." They reached the classroom and Aria sighed. "Great. A whole hour of not understanding a word."

Rosa patted her on the shoulder. "I will help you understand, I promise."

"Thank you," Aria said, brightening up.

They entered the classroom and took their seats, and Aria grinned at Shelly who came in late after them.

"Hello, Heart Chakra group. Today, we are going to focus on how it is possible to change environmental laws," Miracle announced, turning to refer to a very complicated chart on the screen behind him.

Aria groaned inwardly, but forced herself to pay attention. She hoped Rosa would decode it all for her later. As much as she wanted to change the world, she had to admit, all she wanted to do was to paint, dance, and be amongst the trees.

She hoped there would be time to play when she finally got to Earth.

CHAPTER FIFTEEN

The next ten years at the Academy slipped by so quickly that Emerald couldn't quite believe it. They had got into a comfortable, if not hectic, routine of classes and activities, and each day had blurred into the next, month after month slipping by, until suddenly Emerald realised it had been a whole decade since she and Mica had gone back through the mists to the Academy.

"It feels like it's all been, a bit, well, easy," Emerald commented to Mica as they woke up for yet another day of classes. There were more rest periods now, as rest and relaxation classes had been introduced when it became clear that the Earth Angels were on the verge of information overload and burning out, a few years previously.

"Easy? Which bit, exactly?" Mica teased. "It's been a lot of hard work. Although, the lying has got easier. We've been here so long, it's difficult to remember the old timeline. It feels like this is the only reality now."

"I mean, when we were at the Academy before, there seemed to be so much doubt, and fear, and then there were the surprises, like the Golden Age Children and second years arriving, and the professors returning to earth, and Laguz coming back..."

Mica lifted himself up onto one elbow and grinned down at Emerald. "Are you... bored?"

Emerald chuckled. "No, not bored, just… surprised. I assumed there would be more drama, more resistance to the changes."

"More excitement?"

"Yeah, I suppose so. Oh, I don't know. It just feels like it has all gone off without a hitch, and I guess there's a human part of me that's waiting for things to go wrong."

Mica leaned down to kiss his Flame. "I love that there's a part of you that's still human. But please don't manifest trouble just to appease your boredom. If you want some fun, we could always try to access the Leprechaun Garden again."

Emerald smiled. "I'm sorry. I won't focus on things going wrong. I just had this weird feeling when I woke up, that's all. I'm sure it will go away."

"Good." Mica glanced over at the two walls covered in their notes. "You know, perhaps you are right though. Perhaps it is time to change things a little?"

Emerald frowned. "Haven't we already changed everything possible?"

"I was thinking the other day about how we are teaching the Earth Angels all this information, yet they have no way of putting it into practice until they get to Earth. Unless..."

Emerald raised an eyebrow. "Unless?"

"We make some additions to the Academy. Like a town. With shops, and a bank, a post office and other businesses."

"Create a town in the Academy? So the Earth Angels could have jobs and earn money and then manage it?"

"Yes, exactly. So they have actual experience of what it's like to live on Earth, make a living, budget. We could even have a council? And they could pay taxes and elect people? That might make politics easier to understand, I have heard that some of the trainees have struggled with it."

Emerald smiled at her Flame. "I think this is a fantastic idea! They could actually use the information we have given them! Are you going to approach Velvet about it?"

Mica kissed her and nodded. He then glanced at the clock on the wall and groaned. "I better get up. My first class starts in ten minutes. I will visit Velvet afterward, and put forth the idea."

"Let me know what she says. My first class isn't until a bit later. I was going to go for a walk in the gardens this morning."

Mica threw back the covers and got up, stretching and yawning. "Okay, have a restful morning. I'll see you back here later."

"Sure."

Somehow, despite her excitement about the new idea, Emerald fell asleep again, waking up two hours later, leaving her only half an hour to go for a walk. She got up and headed to the Atlantis Garden. She didn't know why she kept feeling a pull to visit there, especially now that without Laguz's statue, it no longer held the Twin Flame energy. But she still had the weird feeling that she couldn't shake, and now that she was stood before the dolphin statue, it was getting stronger.

She sat on the bench and closed her eyes, hoping to meditate and calm her mind before her class, which was on self-esteem.

"Hello."

Emerald gasped. She knew that voice. She slowly opened her eyes and turned to look at the soul sat next to her. When his emerald green eyes met her own, her heart plummeted to her feet and the weird feeling she'd had all morning suddenly made sense.

"Hello, Laguz."

*　*　*

"You called, Corduroy?"

Velvet approached her old friend. He was sat in the Angelic Garden, on the golden bench in front of the waterfall.

Corduroy looked up at her and smiled. "Yes, please join me."

Velvet sat beside him and breathed in the scent of a nearby jasmine plant. "I should spend more time in this garden, it's beautiful."

"Yes, you should. Especially now that you have increased the rest periods. And about time too, I feared we were going to create an army of workaholic Earth Angels."

Velvet laughed. "I was afraid too, which is why I thought that bringing in the therapies and exercise and rest periods would be a good idea. We can't have all the trainees burning out before they even reach Earth."

"Yes, that would be a bad idea."

There were a few moments of silence between them, and all Velvet could hear was the water hitting the smooth rock below the falls, and the distant chatter of the trainees enjoying their time off.

"I'm not coming with you," Corduroy said.

Velvet looked at her friend, his head was bowed. "To Earth? You wish to remain here?"

Corduroy looked up at her and nodded. "Yes. I think I need to sit this one out, and let you fly solo."

Velvet could hear the attempt at a joke, but his voice sounded too bleak for it to be funny. "Why?"

Corduroy looked at the falls, and sighed. "Because I think you would be happier without me this time. And because I can help you more from here. Whenever you see a black crow, you will know I am with you, guiding you."

Velvet reached out and placed her hand on his knee. He put his hand over hers and squeezed it.

"I will miss you," she said.

"No, you won't, you will be too busy saving the world." Corduroy smiled at her, but it came off as more of a grimace.

"I'm not going yet," Velvet said. "We still have time."

"And for that I am eternally grateful."

Velvet shifted over and leaned her head on the Professor of Death's shoulder. The soft fabric of his robes rubbed against her cheek. "So many changes, so many new things to comprehend. I feel both excited and nervous about all that is yet to come."

"It will be the best adventure yet, I promise." Corduroy patted her hand then stood up, and Velvet looked up at him, sure that she could see tears gathering in his eyes. "I must go. Thank you for meeting with me. I will see you later."

Velvet nodded and Corduroy disappeared. She sighed. She felt sad that her next life would not be with one of her oldest friends. They had been through so much together. Feeling a bit stiff, she decided to go for a walk, and without meaning to, found herself in the Atlantis Garden. She saw Emergence was there, deep in conversation with a man with long blonde hair. She frowned. He looked familiar. Before she could move closer to get a better look at his face, both he and Emergence disappeared.

Feeling disappointed but not really understanding why, Velvet decided to return to her office to prepare her lessons for the afternoon. She made a mental note to ask the Oracle later who the man was, then she clicked her fingers and disappeared.

*   *   *

"Hey, Emerald, I managed to see Velvet earlier and-"

"Miracle, we have a visitor."

Mica's eyes widened when he saw Emerald in their room with a very familiar soul. "Laguz! Um, oh, hi!"

"Emerald?" Laguz frowned and looked at her. "You said your name was Emergence? What is going on here?"

Mica shot his Flame a look. He noticed that she had masked their notes and everything on the walls, and he wondered how to respond.

Emerald sighed. "It's no good, Mica. I have tried to dissuade him, but I think we should tell him the truth. He has come here looking for Velvet."

"Oh," Mica said, slumping into the chair by the desk.

"Why is that such a bad thing? We are Flames. I love her. She loves me."

"But she has forgotten that," Emerald said gently.

"I figured out that much, but why should I not remind her?" Laguz asked, frowning.

"Because everything we are trying to do here hinges on her bad memory." Mica waved his hand to remove the mask, and their two walls of notes, charts, diagrams, sketches and ideas appeared.

Laguz gasped, his eyes darting over everything, trying to comprehend what it all was. "I don't understand, maybe you could explain it to me?"

Mica sighed and began to explain that they were posing as Oracles from the Thirteenth Dimension to change the course of the world. He didn't mention that they had already lived the path once already, he just said they had been given a vision.

"And you think that if Velvet remembers me, and the Flames reunite, then all this," Laguz pointed at the walls, "Will be for nothing?"

"We do not think that, we *know* that. We believe that the Twin Flames do not reunite when an age is about to end, but that the reunion of the Flames is what causes it to end. And this new path means that there will not be an ending. We will have changed it long before it gets to that point, taking us into a brand new reality."

"The Diamond Age?"

Emerald frowned. "Yes, how did you know it was called that?"

"There have been whispers throughout the dimensions. It reached us in the Seventh. That is why I came, I thought maybe Velvet was behind it."

"No, it was us. It's interesting that the ripples of what we are doing here is reaching other dimensions though." Mica looked at Laguz. "We have been here for ten years, training the Earth Angels to be able to thrive and really make a difference on Earth. If Velvet sees you now, it will all be over. We will be headed for the same fate that we Saw."

Laguz was quiet for a moment as he studied some of their notes. "Was it really so terrible? That version of reality?"

Mica looked at Emerald, who looked like she was going to cry. "It wasn't awful, and there were some bright moments, but they were short-lived. And the world as a whole would decline to the point of being unable to support human life."

Laguz sighed. "That doesn't sound great."

"It's not," Emerald said. "If it had been great, we would have allowed it to continue."

Laguz looked at her. "Continue?"

Mica shot her a look as well. She shook her head. "I mean, we wouldn't have intervened at this stage, we would have let it unfurl as it was in our vision."

Laguz looked unconvinced by her explanation but didn't question her further.

"Laguz, we understand your desire to see Velvet, we really do. But if you want what is best for her, and for every other soul on Earth, then you will return to the Seventh Dimension, and you will assist her from there if needed, but not until she is on Earth."

"I have already spent what feels like an eternity without her," Laguz whispered. "Waiting for her to call me to her."

Emerald reached out to hug him. "Then the next hundred years will go by in a flash. When she returns from Earth, we promise that she will be directed straight to you."

"A hundred years?"

Laguz's expression broke Mica's heart. "She won't go to Earth for another twenty years yet, and we believe that if all goes to plan she will be at least eighty years old before she comes home again."

Laguz closed his eyes and took a deep breath. "I understand." He stood there for a while, and Mica glanced at Emerald, who was doing her best to maintain her composure.

After a few moments, Laguz reached up to remove the leather cord from around his neck. He looked at the wooden pendant on it, then handed it to Mica. "Can you make sure she gets this the moment she comes home? It will lead her straight to me."

Mica took it, and glanced down at the rune burned into the smooth wood. He nodded at Laguz. "I will, I promise."

Laguz nodded then smiled at Emerald. "Thank you, I will leave now, and I promise I will not interfere. And I will let the souls in the Seventh Dimension know what is happening."

"Thank you for understanding," Mica said, putting the pendant in his robe pocket for safe keeping. "We both promise that we will protect and assist Velvet."

"I should go," Laguz whispered. Emerald hugged him, then with one last look at Mica, Laguz disappeared.

Mica exhaled loudly and looked at his Flame who was now openly crying. "Enough drama and excitement for you?" he tried to joke.

Emerald smiled but it turned into a sob, and Mica crossed the room in two strides to wrap his arms around her. His heart hurt for Laguz. If he had to wait a hundred years to be with Emerald he didn't think he would be able to cope.

"Are you *sure* this is the right path?" Emerald whispered when her sobs had subsided.

"I don't know," Mica said honestly, tears filling his own eyes. "But it is the path we have committed to. So let's see it through."

CHAPTER SIXTEEN

When the voice first called his name, Tm was convinced that one of his roommates must have arrived back, but he was alone in the room, and the door was closed. He frowned. They had been taught what it would be like when the Angels called them forth to their earthly life, but it had only been ten years, and he was just a first year. Surely the second years would be called back before him?

He closed his eyes and lay back on his bed. He tried to meditate, but it wasn't long before the voice called him again, and this time it was a little louder. It definitely sounded like an Angel. He sat up and looked around the room, which had gone through many different styles of décor over the last decade, thanks to the little green Faerie who had a very short attention span.

Was this it? Was he going to Earth?

His heart both leapt and constricted at the thought. He had not heard from Au since he sent the light message. By his calculations, it was likely she hadn't even received it yet. But he had hoped to be at the Academy long enough for her to receive it and maybe find a faster way to reply.

But when the voice called out again, he knew that he would not be.

He knew how to answer the call, but he didn't want to leave without seeing his friends, and without alerting the professors to the fact that he had been called.

He got up and left the room, and made his way through the corridors to the offices of the Academy. He reached Velvet's office, and hoped it wasn't too late an hour to be calling.

He raised his hand to knock and the door disappeared before he could, as though he was expected.

"Thank you for coming, Emergence," Velvet said without looking up as he entered the sparsely decorated office. Tm frowned and cleared his throat.

"I'm afraid I am not Emergence. My name is Tm."

Velvet looked up. "Oh! My apologies, I was expecting the Oracle. Dear Starperson, what can I do for you?"

Tm moved closer to her desk. "I have been called. And I wanted to let you know."

Velvet gasped. "Called? To Earth?"

There was a knock at the door, and Velvet waved her hand to open it. Emergence stepped in, smiled at Velvet, and then looked at Tm in confusion. "Oh, I'm sorry, am I interrupting?"

"This trainee has been called, Emergence," Velvet said, shock still evident on her face.

"Oh!" Emergence said, looking at Tm. "You can hear the call now?"

Tm nodded. "It's not very loud yet, but it is increasing in urgency, just as you described."

"Do you feel ready?" Velvet asked him.

Tm sighed. "Yes. I had hoped to hear from home before

going, but I do feel ready to step into my human incarnation, and use my knowledge to assist with the Awakening."

Velvet smiled at him. "You are a beautiful soul who will no doubt make a huge difference. Thank you for volunteering."

Tm smiled back. "I could not watch and do nothing. I must go and say goodbye to my friends before I answer the call."

Velvet stood up and went over to him. She wrapped her arms around him, surprising Tm with a strong hug. He hugged the Old Soul back.

"I have a feeling we will meet again," she said. "Until then, much love and luck to you."

Tm nodded. He smiled at the Oracle, then left the office to find the crazy green Faerie. To say goodbye, and to ask her a favour.

*　*　*

"What was it you needed, Velvet?" Emerald asked a few moments after Tm left.

Velvet looked at her, and frowned, as if she had forgotten why she had called. "Oh," she said after a moment. "Yes, I saw you with a soul in the Atlantis Garden earlier today, and I wondered who it was."

Emerald's eyes widened, and she thought quickly. "Oh, that was just a messenger," she said in what she hoped was a dismissive tone.

Velvet sat behind her desk. "A messenger? He looked familiar."

"Yes, a messenger," Emerald said, stalling while she thought of a suitable message. "From the Thirteenth

Dimension. He was bringing news that the trainees were about to be called to Earth."

Velvet raised an eyebrow. "But you seemed surprised when I said Tm had been called?"

"Only because I assumed the second years would be called first," Emerald said quickly. "The messenger, um, didn't specify who would be called."

"Oh. Okay. I don't know why he seemed familiar." Velvet shook her head. "Did the messenger have any further news?"

Emerald shook her head. "No, that was all. Everything is going according to plan."

"I see. That's good."

Emerald watched Velvet sort things on her desk for a moment, trying to discern whether the Old Soul would suddenly realise why she recognised Laguz. But then she looked up at her and smiled.

"I love Miracle's suggestion about the town. I have already spoken with the other professors, and they are busy designing it at the moment. Giving the trainees practical ways to learn this new material is brilliant. I think it will be very successful."

"Yes, Miracle does have some wonderful ideas, and I agree with you. I think it will be very helpful," Emerald agreed, relieved with the abrupt change in subject.

Velvet nodded. "I apologise for calling you here unnecessarily, I will let you get back to whatever you were doing."

Emerald nodded at the dismissal and retreated, heading back to where Mica awaited her in their room. She still felt a heaviness in her heart from their visit from Laguz, and from having to lie to Velvet. She thought of the moment at the Twin Flame Retreat when Velvet had returned from the stars, and Laguz had come to find her. She thought of the song that had brought their souls together, and tears fell down her cheeks. Until Velvet returned from Earth again, in a hundred years' time, she would not remember her Flame, and even then, she would perhaps never remember the moments she spent in Laguz's arms on Earth, and the life they created together there.

Emerald reached her room and entered, to find Mica writing at the desk. He looked up at her and saw her tears. He stood up and went to her, she melted into his embrace, and he sighed. "What did she want?"

"Velvet saw Laguz, earlier, in the gardens. I managed to convince her that he was a messenger and nothing more."

Mica pulled back a little to look at her. "What did you say the message was?"

Emerald explained what had happened with Tm just before, and how she used that to furnish her lie.

"The Earth Angels are being called? Wow. I thought we would have more time."

"So did I. But I think we have taught them a lot in the last ten years. It's a shame he is leaving before having the practical training, but Tm was an excellent trainee. I have no doubt he will Awaken, and make a difference."

Mica nodded. He gently wiped her wet face with his handkerchief. "Are you okay?"

Emerald sighed. "I fear that sometime soon we may also be called. And I am just not ready to lose you yet."

"You can never lose me. You know that. And besides, we won't leave until we are certain that we have taught the Earth Angels everything we know. So we have time yet."

"In that case, can we go to the Leprechaun Garden? I

need a little laughter to lift my spirits."

Mica chuckled. "Yes, of course."

* * *

"Oh, Tim! I'm so excited for you! I can't believe you're going to Earth! Of course I promise to do that for you, I won't let you down."

Tm smiled at Aria. "Thank you, I really appreciate it. Being called is very strange, I hadn't expected to go so soon, but I am looking forward to it." He reached out to hug her, then stepped back. "I will see you there." He closed his eyes to answer the call, when he felt a small hand on his arm. He opened his eyes again to see Aria frowning at him.

"You can't just leave! What about your leaving party?"

Tm laughed. "Leaving party?"

"We don't get leaving parties?" Aria said, shocked. "That's terrible! We should be celebrating!" She took his hand and pulled him down the path to the Elemental Garden. She reached the centre where a delicate bell hung on the end of a curved pole. She grabbed the cord and rang the bell a bit too enthusiastically, making Tm put his hands over his ears.

"Tim is leaving for Earth!" Aria cried out. "Let's celebrate!"

Several trainees nearby came towards them, clapping and cheering, and before he knew it, Tm was surrounded by souls hugging him and chanting his name. He blushed a deep red at the attention, and though he wished he could have just left quietly as planned, he knew that Aria had meant well in her bid to say farewell.

Someone started playing music, and the trainees all began dancing, and Tm joined in, forgetting for a moment that he had to leave this beautiful place so soon.

After a while though, he could hear the Angels calling him again, even over the noise of the impromptu party, and he stopped dancing and made his way through the crowd to find his Faerie friend. She was dancing with Shelly when he found her. He tapped her on the shoulder and she turned to grin at him.

"It's time," he shouted over the din.

Aria nodded, and hugged him tightly. "I will keep my promise to you. Take care, Alien."

"Thank you. I will."

He stepped back, and saw that the Faerie had tears in her eyes. He gave her the blue handkerchief from his pocket, and she took it and wiped her face.

Tm smiled, closed his eyes, and answered the call.

*   *   *

Starlight approached the shimmering golden castle, wondering if she was doing the right thing, but knowing that she would always wonder if she didn't try. She had waited longer than she had originally intended to seek the help of the Indigo Children, but now that the trainees were being called to Earth, it felt like it was time.

She dismissed the errant thought that perhaps she should have checked with the Oracles first. She was still, after all, the Angel of Destiny, and therefore it was still her decision to make, not theirs.

She waited before the gates, and sent her greetings telepathically to the Indigo Child within. Moments later, the gates opened, and she flew up the path towards the doorway. Before she reached it, the doors opened and a blue sphere of light zoomed out and transformed into a beautiful Child who stood before her, a frown on her face.

Starlight frowned too. This was not the greeting she had been expecting.

"Starlight, what is happening?" the tiny Child asked, her voice sad.

"Whatever do you mean, dear Indigo?"

"Someone has changed the timelines, haven't they?"

Starlight's eyes widened. "But how can you tell? From all the way out here?" The Indigo world was as far from Earth as it was possible to be. It wasn't even in the same galaxy.

"Of course we can tell. Just a few years ago we were on Earth, living human lives, and now, we are back here. Ripped away from our families and our lives there. My brothers and sisters are much aggrieved, and it has brought a darkness to our world."

"Ripped away? I don't understand," Starlight said, her mind a chaotic whirl. "You were on Earth? But how?"

The Child looked up at her in wonder. "You really don't know, do you? I can see that in your confusion. Please, where are my manners? Come in."

Starlight followed the Child into the castle, and noticed along the way that the Indigos she passed were indeed darker in colour, and as they reached the balcony overlooking the city, she could feel a heavy energy lingering.

Once they were seated, Starlight spoke.

"Please explain to me, dear Indigo, what you mean. I have come seeking your help, to ask you to go to Earth. I don't understand how you could have already been there?"

"This is a new timeline. In the old one you already asked us to go, and we did. We attended the School for the Children of the Golden Age, and then we were called to Earth, often becoming the children of the Earth Angels already called there. We grew up, some of us even had our own families, and then in the blink of an eye, one day in the 2020s, we were back here again."

Starlight shook her head. "You mean someone went back in time and changed things? Bringing you back here?"

The Indigo Child sighed. "I do not know how it happened. All I know is, we have spent much time since, mourning the loss of our lives there, and waiting impatiently for you to visit us, so we can return."

Starlight sat back, feeling stunned. Suddenly, it was all beginning to fall into place. "The Oracles," she whispered, mostly to herself. She looked at the Indigo Child. "I am so sorry for the loss and the trauma, but…" she couldn't believe she was about to defend them, but the glorious vision of the new world flashed back through her mind, and she knew that she needed to do whatever it would take to make it happen. "I do feel that they meant well by their actions, and would never have meant to cause you any harm."

The Indigo Child did not look convinced.

"Tell me, what was the world like? In the 2020s?" Starlight asked.

The Indigo Child was quiet for a few moments. "Why?"

"Was it the best possible reality it could be? Were the Earth Angels following their purpose? Was it a happy place?" Starlight was really hoping she would say no, otherwise her argument was moot.

The Child sighed. "No, it was not. It was still full of hate, and war, and crime. It had improved, but not by much. Despite that, it was still where our families were, and those we loved."

Starlight nodded, relieved but also a bit sad. "Again, I am so sorry, but I do believe that the ones who instigated this change in timeline did so because they believed it could be better, and I have Seen it. I have Seen the world they are seeking to create, and it is really something to behold. If you wish to return to Earth, then travel with your kin to the Earth Angel Training Academy. The professors there will teach you all you need to know to create this world."

The Child frowned. "Last time, we were taught by two Faeries, Linen and Aria. Will that not be so this time?"

"Faerie teachers?" Starlight shook her head. "No, you will learn from the Old Souls and the Oracles alongside the Earth Angels. The Oracles are the ones who have brought about the changes, and they have brought with them knowledge that will create this new world. I believe that if you listen to them, you will not only be with your loved ones again on Earth, but you will live a far more joyful existence in a world with peace, love, and community."

The Child stood up and stared out over her city. "I will have to ask my siblings. I will not force them to go, it must be their choice. Some have only just begun to recover, and it is a lot to ask, as they may possibly suffer such loss again."

Starlight stood up. "I appreciate that. And I appreciate you trusting me."

The Child looked up at her. "I can see the truth in your eyes. And I do trust you." She smiled. "I wish to see this new world, and I wish to see my family again. So I will be there, you have my word."

Starlight bowed her head. "Thank you."

"Will you call upon the Crystals, Rainbows and Diamonds too?"

Starlight frowned. "Diamonds?"

"Yes. Last time, I know you called forth the Rainbows and Crystals, but we have been made aware of a new world in our galaxy, where the Diamond Children reside. We assumed it was all part of the change in the timeline."

Starlight smiled at the Indigo. "I think I might just have to pay them a visit, thank you for telling me about them."

"Of course," the Child replied, looking a little puzzled. "What would the Diamond Age be without the Diamond Children?"

CHAPTER SEVENTEEN

"They remember?"

Emerald's hand flew to her mouth, and she looked as aghast as Mica felt.

"We had no idea," he told Starlight. "We assumed everyone would forget and simply revert to their previous incarnations. Are they okay?"

Starlight sighed. "They have been deeply affected by it, but I think once they experience the new world, they will understand."

"I guess this answers Magenta's question on where the souls from the second timeline are now," Mica said to Emerald, who still appeared to be in shock.

"What I would like to know," Starlight said, looking at them both. "Is who *are* you? Really?"

Emerald and Mica exchanged glances. The list of people who knew the truth was getting longer, and it was cause for concern. What if one of them let it slip to Velvet?

Mica sighed and looked down at the cloudy mist swirling around his feet. "We are not Oracles, we are not from the Thirteenth Dimension. We are Angels. I am Mica," he looked at Emerald. "And this is Emerald. We were second year trainees at the Academy the first time round, and we went to Earth. Our mission was to reunite the Flames."

Starlight narrowed her eyes. "The Twin Flames? I knew it! I knew there was something missing."

"Yes, in our timeline, the Flames were reuniting, but it wasn't helping the Earth Angels with their missions, it was hindering them. Both Mica and I had already returned home when Magenta also came home and asked us to go back in time and change everything, because of a vision she had." Emerald reached out and took Mica's hand, and he squeezed it gently.

"You did all of this on the order of a Seer?" Starlight asked, her tone incredulous. "Why didn't you consult with an Elder? Or me?"

"You were on Earth, as was Gold."

"I was on Earth?" It was Starlight's turn to be shocked.

"Yes. You went to Earth to help Velvet, and you had two children. Gold followed you there, and you were together." Emerald squeezed his hand tightly and he glanced at her. She closed her eyes and shook her head slightly. When he saw that Starlight was crying, he realised that maybe he had revealed too much.

"I had children and my Flame by my side in this timeline, and you decided to change it?"

Mica tried not to wince, but he could sense her anger building. He needed to diffuse it, quickly. "Magenta lost her Flame too. Many of the Earth Angels will have lost much, as did the Indigos, but you have Seen the world we could create. It is far superior to the world as it was, I can assure you. If we had not done this, then the world would have surely ended within another few decades. And even if it didn't end it wouldn't have been a truly happy place to live. The way humans were living was completely unsustainable. They isolated themselves through technology, they destroyed the Elemental Realm in their need for material wealth, and though it appeared as though they had everything, they were still miserable."

Emerald stepped forward and reached out to touch Starlight's arm. "Our hearts broke at the thought of the Flames not being together, and we have questioned our path many times, but ultimately, for the good of all, this really is the best way for the planet."

Mica and Emerald waited quietly while Starlight appeared to be having an internal debate. He hoped they would be able to win her over to their point of view, otherwise she could expose them and it would all be over.

"I don't know if I would agree with your actions, which is why I assume you did not seek higher permission. It would have been too difficult to get. But I have Seen the world you are creating, and it is beautiful, and I would like to see it come to pass. Therefore, I will put my faith and trust in you, but only if you do not lie to me again."

The two Angels nodded quickly. "You have our word. We will be truthful to you. But only if you promise not to tell anyone else of this. If Velvet finds out about the Flames then they will reunite and our plans will be ruined."

Starlight nodded. "I can do that. I will keep it to myself."

"Thank you," Mica said with relief. "We know it's difficult to keep such big secrets. Now, I'm sorry to run but I am aware we have classes."

"I have one more question before you go," Starlight said before the Angels could turn away.

"Yes?" Mica asked.

"How did you know about the Diamond Children?"

Mica frowned and looked at Emerald, who also looked confused. "The what?"

"You called this new age the Diamond Age, and there are currently Children on a planet in another galaxy called the Diamond Children. I went to visit them after I visited the Indigos, Crystals and Rainbows. They are highly evolved beings who are ready to go to Earth to create this new world of yours. But if all you did was go back in time, how did you know about them?"

When Mica and Emerald were silent for a few moments, she prompted them. "The truth, please."

Emerald shook her head. "The truth is, we had no idea. When we came back, we were making everything up as we went along. And when it came to it, I didn't want to mention the Golden Age, which is what we were previously trying to create, because I was afraid it would trigger memories. So I made up the Diamond Age." She shrugged. "It sounded good."

Starlight raised an eyebrow. "You made it up?"

Emerald nodded. "Yes. I just said the first thing that came to me. I had no idea that there were actually Diamond Children."

"Me neither. Do you think that our actions have created them? Or that they existed and were sending us the information?" Mica asked.

"I have no idea," Starlight replied. "But they are powerful, and I think that with their help we will most certainly create the Diamond Age."

Emerald smiled. "We look forward to meeting them. Will they come here first?"

Starlight nodded. "Yes, they are making preparations,

along with the Indigos, Crystals and Rainbows."

Emerald looked at Mica, her eyes shining. "A whole light army, isn't that incredible?"

Mica smiled, pleased that Emerald's doubts about the Children coming appeared to have evaporated. "Yes it is. Now I believe we both may be late for our classes?"

"I will keep you informed on their arrival," Starlight said in dismissal. "Please keep me in the loop."

Mica nodded to the Angel of Destiny. "Thank you. We will."

*　*　*

Aria looked down at the coins and bits of coloured paper she held in one hand, and the little bank book she held in the other. She looked at Shelly, her eyes wide. "It was a lot easier to just manifest what we needed."

Shelly chuckled and tucked her money into her shell purse. "I think this is a brilliant idea. Did you see the book shop? It's full of every book imaginable!"

"Yes, but you have to work to earn the money to be able to buy them. Where's the fun in that?" Aria grumbled.

"I'm sure we can find some work that you would enjoy. I saw on the list that there were gardening jobs available."

Aria brightened up a little. Working in the gardens didn't sound so bad. "I wouldn't mind that, I guess. At least I will be able to buy some of those amazing looking bars of chocolate then!"

"I hope you're not planning to spend all your money on snacks," Sapphire commented. "We have to pay for our rooms now, and our food here too."

Aria made a face. "Really? Will there be any money left for fun stuff?"

"I guess we will find that out in our next Finances class with Cotton. She is going to teach us about saving money in our bank accounts, and how to budget."

Aria sighed. "As long as I can buy sweet treats every now and then, I guess I will survive." She tucked the money and banking book into her little toadstool shaped rucksack, and she followed Shelly to the town that had been created for them. Though she was feeling a bit grumpy at having to work, she was quite excited about the new developments.

When they reached the square, she gasped. There was a new shop. She ran over to the window and stared in at all of the art supplies, her mouth open. She had been really enjoying the art classes they had been taking, and she would love to be able to develop it further, maybe even open her own gallery one day...

"I know where my money will be going," she declared to her Mermaid friend.

"And I know where mine will be," Shelly replied, looking into the window of the shop next door, which contained the most beautiful dresses.

"Oh no! Are we going to have to buy clothes now too? Won't anything be free anymore?"

"It's not free on Earth," Shelly reminded her. "And they are trying to prepare us to be able to survive there."

Aria sighed. "This human lark is getting less fun by the second." She stared through the window a few moments longer then sighed again. "Come on, let's go and find out how we're supposed to manage these little metal things."

Shelly laughed at her tone. "Oh, it will be fun, and don't worry, we will find a way for you to afford your art supplies."

"We'd better. Race?"

"You're on!" Shelly darted off before Aria could shout

go, and she ran after her friend, giggling and yelling out -
"Not fair!"

Amethyst hummed while she sewed the pieces of fabric together. She was a little surprised at first when they decided to create a town and ask the trainees to work, earn money and live like humans, but she found that she was actually really enjoying herself. She had chosen to be a seamstress, to make clothing to sell in the clothes shop in the town, which the trainees had dubbed Angelton. She loved making beautiful dresses and robes, as well as more contemporary clothing to match the era on Earth.

She examined her stitching to make sure it was perfect and smiled. Doing a good job made her feel happy, and she knew that it would be really important to do work that she loved when she got to Earth. She never wanted to feel miserable in order to simply earn money.

The bell rang above the door, signalling that someone had come into the shop. She was on her own as the other seamstresses were in classes all afternoon. Amethyst went out to greet the potential customer and when she saw it was the second year she had run into many years before, she blushed.

"Cobalt," she said. "How may I help you?"

He smiled at her. "Amethyst, isn't it?"

She nodded, blushing a deeper shade of red.

Cobalt held up his bright blue robes. "I was wondering if you could help me with this tear. Before, I would have just manifested new robes or fixed these ones magically, but now, I suppose I should pay for you to sew them back up."

Amethyst examined the large tear in the soft fabric. "I should be able to fix that. You will need to slip them off for me."

Cobalt nodded and pulled his robes off over his head, revealing a thin white shirt underneath, and nothing else. Amethyst blushed an even deeper shade of red, and averted her eyes. She took the robes and went to the back where the machines were.

"Thank you," Cobalt called out after her.

She didn't answer. She busied herself with fixing the robes, willing her burning cheeks to cool. It only took her five minutes to fix, and she came back out to find Cobalt examining one of her latest creations. He turned around and she held out the robes, her eyes on the ceiling.

"There, you can't really see the tear anymore. How did you do it, anyway?" she asked, her eyes still averted while he slipped them back on.

"I was helping to build a cabin, in the woods beyond the Elemental Garden, and I caught them on a nail."

"Oh. I see. Well, I'm glad I could help." Amethyst nodded to him and started to return to the back.

"Wait, how much do I owe you?"

"Oh, um, er, just one Angel coin."

Cobalt frowned. "Really? That's not very much. Here," he said, digging into his pocket and pulling out three. He placed them in Amethyst's hand, and again, for no particular reason, she expected there to be a spark, but there was nothing.

"Thank you, I appreciate it."

Amethyst nodded, and watched him leave the shop, the coins still warm in her hand. Why did she feel like there should be a connection to him when there clearly was none?

She shook her head at herself and returned to her work. Within moments, she lost herself in the rhythm of her work and started humming again.

CHAPTER EIGHTEEN

Mica watched the first elections of Angelton Council, and couldn't help but feel proud of the Earth Angel trainees. They had taken to Earth life in the created town with such ease. They understood what it was to work, to manage money, and how the economy worked. They had even learned how do their taxes!

He knew without a doubt that they would find life on Earth so much easier now.

"I hope the Faerie Party win," Emerald whispered in his ear. He glanced at her, eyebrow raised. "Really? There would be no money for the upkeep of the town after all the parties they would throw. You've seen what they have been like with the celebrations every time an Earth Angel is called."

"They do like to have fun, but I think you underestimate them. I think they would take care of the town, and the people."

"You may be right. I must admit, they are very hard workers when they find work they enjoy. But don't you think the Star Party would be better? They really know their figures, and how to run the banks. They would do better with the council budget."

"Honestly? I think they are all amazing."

Mica smiled. "Yes, they are. And with their knowledge of politics, I know they will have a much bigger impact when they get to Earth."

"I agree. They are going to shift everything so much faster." Emerald was quiet for a moment. "Do you think we should look though?"

Mica frowned. "Look?"

"At the world. We haven't been to the lake in the Angelic Realm in such a long time. We could go later, and see what is transpiring on Earth. See if there are already changes?"

Mica nodded. "I can't imagine that much would have changed yet, the Earth Angels we have sent will be merely infants. But I admit it would be nice to have a break from the Academy. It has been so busy here."

"It will be even busier soon. Aren't the Children arriving shortly?"

"I spoke to Starlight about that. I think the Indigos will be here within the year, followed in the next few years by the Crystals, Rainbows and Diamonds."

They were quiet for a few minutes while they listened to the Faerie campaign speech, then Emerald whispered. "I still cannot believe the Diamond Children actually exist."

"I can." He kissed her on the cheek. "I've always thought you were a bit psychic."

Emerald chuckled softly. "I think I just got lucky on that one."

"Maybe."

They watched the rest of the elections, and then when the time came, they stepped forward to vote for the party they wanted to win. Mica voted for the Star Party. He peeked at Emerald's sheet and saw that she had voted for the Faerie Party.

They left the main hall and headed towards the front door to leave the Academy, to visit the Angelic Realm. They avoided going through the main gate, and used their magic to transport themselves to the far edge of the lake. They couldn't risk being seen by the other Angels, as they might recognise them as the Angels they really were, and blow their Oracle cover.

Emerald knelt at the edge of the water and touched the surface lightly. The ripples moved outwards, and then stopped, and the surface of the water became a screen. She sat back and Mica wrapped his arms around her. They watched people on Earth for a while, and could see very subtle changes in people's lives.

"I hope this means it's working," Emerald said.

"Me too. It's only slightly different, but as I said earlier, the Earth Angels we have sent recently are still very young."

"Should we have created a walk-in programme too? To put Earth Angels directly into adult bodies?"

Mica considered the idea for a moment. "It's a thought. Linen and Aria created such a programme didn't they? Did they have success with it?"

Emerald shook her head. "I cannot say that I am sure. But it might be worth considering if there are souls who are happy to come home that have their lives taken on by someone else."

"Might it not just create more disconnection though? Look at what happened with Laguz. He left his wife and two children. Just disappeared one night. That can't have a positive impact."

"You're right. Perhaps it would just complicate things too much. I am being impatient, that's all. I wish to see the changes now, not wait another few decades for them to occur."

"Perhaps you should visit Cotton. You could do with some one-to-one sessions on patience."

Emerald rolled her eyes. "Maybe." She looked back to the lake, and saw movement out of the corner of her eye. She looked up to see an Angel coming towards them, no doubt intrigued by their unannounced presence.

"Time to go," she whispered. She clasped Mica's hand and they left the lake, reappearing back in their room.

"Early night?" Mica suggested, pulling off his robes and yawning.

Emerald nodded and crossed the room to kiss him. "Yes, let's sleep," she said, a sly smile on her face.

* * *

"Goodness, Tartan is going to have a fit."

Corduroy looked up from the pile of ballot slips he was counting and chuckled. "The Faeries are winning by a mile, eh?"

"Yes, they are. And if they had any magic right now, I would have said they had fixed it. But it seems as though everyone just thinks they are the best ones for the job."

"Or they just think it would be the most fun?"

Velvet smiled. "Yes, most likely." She counted out another twenty slips voting for the Faerie Party.

"I have such a good feeling about everything, you know."

Velvet raised her eyebrow at her Old Soul friend. "*You* have a good feeling?"

Corduroy laughed. "I know, it seems like an oxymoron,

the Professor of Death being positive. But I do. All the extra information we're teaching the trainees, and with the star within, and this new town... I really do think that the world will be a completely different place to what it might have been otherwise."

Velvet nodded. "I do too. Are you sure you don't want to come along and experience it?" She saw emotions flit across his face, and something like pain and longing in his eyes. But he shook his head.

"Nah, I can just check in from here. Besides, I have spoken to the Oracles, and they think that I could run a sanctuary here for humans and Earth Angels who have had traumatic deaths. Help them to heal and release any issues before they move on or reincarnate."

"Oh, Corduroy," Velvet said, moved to tears. "That's beautiful." She reached out to touch her friend's hand and he smiled.

"It would nice to be the healer rather than the destroyer, for once."

"I think you will do a wonderful job. I'm so proud of you, my friend."

"Thank you." Corduroy smiled and pulled his hand away to continue sorting the ballots into piles. "You know, I think you are right."

"About what?" Velvet asked, resuming her own counting.

"The Faeries are going to win."

*   *   *

"Guess what I just heard?"

Aria looked up from her painting of her friend Larry, and saw Shelly running into the room.

"What?" she asked, putting her brush into the water

and turning it red. "Has the Faerie Party won?"

"Oh," Shelly said. "I don't know. They haven't announced the winners of the Election yet."

"What is it then?" Aria asked, intrigued.

"There are new souls coming from other galaxies. They are Children, and they are highly evolved," Shelly said, bursting with excitement.

Aria smiled. "Wow, really? They're coming here to go to Earth with us? To help us?"

Shelly nodded and sat on her bed. "Yes! Isn't that incredible?"

"It really is. I wonder what they will be like. How did you find out? I didn't see any announcements." Aria looked over to the noticeboard, but it was empty.

Shelly blushed, her cheeks turning a brighter red than her hair. "I kind of overheard Velvet talking about it with the Oracles. I don't know if it's meant to be public knowledge yet. They said they will be arriving really soon."

Aria grinned. She loved to be the first to get news. "So cool. I wonder when they will announce it properly. I mean, I think everyone would notice if a whole bunch of highly evolved Children were suddenly running about."

Shelly giggled. "I don't know, some of them might not notice."

Aria giggled too. "True." She looked down at her painting and sighed. She felt a sudden pang of longing for her old home in the Elemental Realm. She hoped Larry was alive and well somewhere.

"That's a beautiful picture," Shelly said, coming over to look. She put her hand on Aria's shoulder. "I promise we will do everything possible to save our realms when we get to Earth. I was thinking, actually, that we should plan what we will do, because if we remember everything," Shelly placed her hand on her heart where her star lay within. "Then we will remember our plans and it might speed up our mission."

"That's a great idea!" Aria got out a fresh sheet of paper, and some coloured pens. "First things first, we need a name."

"I was also thinking, we could start it here as a business in Angelton. We could do fundraising events, and make a business plan. It would be like testing it out before we do it on Earth."

"Oh, that's such a wonderful idea! I mean, I still want to paint and maybe sell my paintings, but to actually start our organisation to save the oceans and the trees sounds amazing!"

Shelly pulled up a chair and grinned at Aria. "So what are we going to call it?"

* * *

"I would say 'I told you so' but..."

Emerald looked at Mica and laughed. "They're just celebrating! Which is something I think humans on Earth definitely need to do more often." She held her hand out to him and he looked at it suspiciously. "Let's dance!" she said.

Mica sighed and took her hand, and she pulled him onto the dancefloor that had appeared in the centre of the town square. There were fairy lights and bunting hung up everywhere, making it all look very festive. There were souls of every origin dancing around them, and a rather lively band, with Tartan in the centre, playing the bagpipes, on the small stage.

"You are right, humans don't tend to celebrate enough.

After all, just waking up in the morning should be a cause for celebration."

Emerald laughed and twirled away from him, and he reached out and pulled her back again. Her robes flew out around her, catching the twinkling lights on the sparkling golden threads.

"Promise me that if we find each other on Earth we will laugh more," she said as he pulled her in close and they swayed to the music.

"I promise. We will dance, we will drink, and we will laugh."

Emerald grinned. "In that case, it will be fun."

"Yes it will," Mica agreed. "You don't seem so afraid of going now?"

Emerald shook her head. "No, because I have an idea."

"Oh?" Mica spun them both around a few times until they reached the edge of the dancefloor, then they both sat down on a bench at the edge. He figured it was safe enough to talk there. The music was so loud that he didn't think anyone would overhear. Besides, everyone was too busy dancing and having fun to notice their conversation.

"Yes, I was thinking of what we were talking about a while ago. About creating a walk-in programme, and I had the idea that we should go as walk-ins. Instead of being born. We wouldn't have to go through growing up all over again, and we could be of use straight away."

Mica's eyes widened. "Oh, of course. I hadn't really thought of that. It makes perfect sense."

"I thought so," Emerald said, feeling pleased that he agreed with her. "We could choose to swap places with two souls who already know each other, and then we have a better chance of being together."

Mica frowned. "Are you still worried that us being together might ruin things? Because we are Flames?"

"I'm not. I don't believe our reunion will trigger other reunions because we are not Velvet. It would only happen if Velvet remembered Laguz. At least, I hope that's the case."

They watched the dancing for a while before Mica spoke again. "It's funny, I was thinking about that the other day, and you know I asked Corduroy and some of the other professors to stay here?"

"Yes?"

"I think they are actually Gods."

When Emerald stared at him blankly, he continued.

"The Old Souls. They are like the Greek Gods. Corduroy is Ares, the God of War, Laguz is Poseidon, God of the Sea, Velvet is Aphrodite, Goddess of Love..."

"Oh," Emerald breathed. "Do you really think so?"

"Yes I do. And I believe that if the God of War is not on Earth, perhaps the new world will be calmer."

"You would hope so. Although," Emerald frowned. "If Athena is in fact Athena, then isn't she the Goddess of War? Should we not be asking her to sit this one out too?"

"Already have," Mica said with a smile. "I had the feeling that she would be needed here, even before this revelation occurred to me."

Emerald shook her head. "You really are brilliant." Mica chuckled, and they watched the festivities for a while longer. Emerald particularly enjoyed watching Velvet and Corduroy dancing the quick-step, completely out of time to the music and the other dancers around them. She watched the Old Soul laugh as her white hair flew around her, and smiled. Despite Emerald's fears of causing her pain by not allowing her to remember her Flame, it would seem that the Old Soul was flourishing regardless. She knew that she would become a powerful woman when she grew up on Earth. As long as she remembered to connect to her star within.

"Penny for them," Mica said, holding out an Angel coin. Emerald took it from him and put it in her pocket. She looked back at Velvet on the dancefloor.

"I was just thinking about Velvet, and how she seems happy. Even without Laguz. And I was thinking that this crazy plan of ours might just work after all."

"It's not crazy, and it *will* work. We will create this new world. The Diamond Age."

Emerald nestled into his side and he wrapped his arm around her. "I can't wait to see it."

"Me neither."

* * *

Several months after the festivities of the first election, Velvet looked upon the Golden City that had appeared in one of the Academy classrooms, her heart full of joy for the beautiful blue spheres of light that were lined up before her. They transformed into radiant Children before her eyes, and she heard Emergence sigh softly next to her. She glanced sideways at the Oracle, who had tears silently trickling down her cheeks.

"They're stunning," Emergence whispered to the Old Soul. Velvet nodded in response. She turned to the smallest Child, who had stepped forward.

"Greetings, Indigo Children. Welcome to the Earth Angel Training Academy."

The Child bowed her head slightly. "Thank you, Velvet. You were expecting us?"

"Yes," Velvet said with a smile. "I was told that you

would need accommodation and that you would be joining the Earth Angel trainees in their classes."

The Child nodded. "That is correct, quite a different experience to..." the Child's eyes widened and she glanced at Emergence.

"To what?" Velvet asked, confused by the expression on the Child's face.

"Oh, um, to how we imagined. The Academy," the Child said, her tiny cheeks going slightly rosy.

Velvet smiled reassuringly. "We hope you are able to acclimatise. We are very excited to have you here with us."

The Child bowed her head again. "We are excited to be here too."

Despite her words, Velvet felt that the Child wasn't being entirely truthful. She certainly didn't sound like she was very excited.

"Shall we follow you to our rooms?"

Velvet shook herself out of her thoughts and nodded. "Yes, please do, they are ready for you."

She and Emergence led the way out of room 333, to the wing that had been created especially for the Indigo Children. She was so glad that the Oracles had warned her of their arrival. It would have been embarrassing had they not been prepared. It had also meant she was able to soundproof the room they arrived into, protecting everyone at the Academy from the very high-pitched noise that the Golden City had created when it entered the Academy. It was very unpleasant to the ear.

They took their time taking the Children to their rooms and settling them in. She made sure they all knew how to manifest what they needed. Then she left them to explore and relax. They would begin their lessons the following day.

Velvet made her way back to her office, saying goodbye to Emergence at the entrance to the gardens.

Back in her sanctuary, Velvet settled into her chair and sighed. She still experienced feelings of déjà vu occasionally, and standing in front of the Golden City of the Indigo Children was the strongest one she'd had in a few years. She recalled the Child's comments and wondered if she somehow knew that they had also done this all before in another timeline. She wasn't sure how that would be possible, however, seeing as no one else remembered.

Velvet sighed. She didn't want to ask in case it stirred up bad memories of the timeline that went horribly wrong. It would be better for all concerned if she kept her feelings of déjà vu to herself, she was sure.

She turned her attention to her notes on the desk, and skimmed through the ones she had taken in one of Miracle's Politics classes. It was a subject that she admitted she knew nothing about previously, but she could understand why the knowledge would be very useful on Earth. After all, how could they change the systems without understanding how the systems worked? It made perfect sense, and Velvet wondered why they hadn't been teaching these subjects long ago. Perhaps the previous timeline wouldn't have gone wrong if they had.

Not that she could change it now. The path they were on seemed to be the best one possible, and Velvet knew that her own path within it would emerge in time. So far, all she had was Magenta's prediction of her being in a position of authority. If that was the case, she needed to learn everything she possibly could to make sure she played her part well.

According to the Oracles, the fate of the world may indeed depend on it.

CHAPTER NINETEEN

"I can show you, little one."

The Indigo Child looked up at Amethyst and smiled in relief. "Oh, thank you, Angel. This Academy is so big! And everything is white. They should consider having coloured hallways so we can more easily identify where we are."

Amethyst nodded and guided the Indigo to their next class, which was Patience 100000001.

"I think that is an excellent idea, you should mention it to the Faerie Council. I think they would love changing the Academy into a rainbow of colour."

The Indigo nodded. "I will do just that. It's all so weird. It wasn't like this before. It's taking some getting used to."

"Before? Have you been to the Academy before?"

The Child blushed a little, and Amethyst was curious. "Oh, no I haven't, but our siblings have, and they reported back to us what it was like. There was no town, no council, and they were not expected to go to classes."

"Of course," Amethyst said, as they reached Cotton's classroom. "It has even changed quite considerably to the beginning of term. I think the Oracles are behind it, they only arrived just before the term started.”

“Oh yes, the Oracles.” The Indigo Child’s face darkened a little, but before Amethyst could think anything of it, Cotton was beginning the class. Amethyst helped the Child throughout the class, explaining anything she didn’t understand, and helping her with the exercises. It felt good to assist someone, to make their life a bit easier. That was what Angels were created to do, after all.

Amethyst noticed Cotton observing them both a couple of times, but thought nothing of it. At the end of the class, she compared her schedule with the Indigo Child’s, and found that they had a very similar schedule, so she offered to walk her to their next class, which was Cause and Effect.

She really enjoyed the Child’s company, and hoped they would be able to spend more time together.

At the end of the day, she ran into Holly and some of the other Faeries on the council.

“Oh, Holly, I have a suggestion for you, from an Indigo Child.” She explained the idea of colour-coding the hallways to make the Academy easier to navigate for the Children, and Holly’s face lit up.

“I love it! What a wonderful idea! I still get lost sometimes, and I have been here for a long time.” Holly grinned at the Angel. “I will put it forward as a suggestion at our next meeting tomorrow. Thank you!”

Amethyst smiled. “Brilliant, I think it will be very helpful.”

“Will I see you at the evening activity later?” Holly asked.

“I think I will retire to my room,” Amethyst said, recalling that the evening activity included loud music. “Have fun.”

Holly laughed. "Will do!" She gave Amethyst a little wave, then danced away to join her Faerie friends.

Amethyst headed back to her room, taking a leisurely stroll through the gardens on the way. She found herself in the Angelic Garden, and spotted a familiar soul in bright blue robes sitting on the bench next to another soul in black.

For no good reason, she found herself moving close enough to hear their conversation.

"I shall miss you, Cobalt," the soul in black said, her voice shaking.

Cobalt touched her cheek, and Amethyst felt a jolt of an unfamiliar emotion run through her.

"My dear Lacy, all you need to do to remember me is to go within. I will be waiting for you when you get to Earth."

"Do you promise?" Lacy asked. Amethyst could see tears on the Old Soul's cheeks, but instead of feeling sympathy or pity, the Angel felt anger.

"I promise. Now, I must answer the call. It is getting too loud to bear."

"Of course, I will see you there."

Cobalt leaned in to kiss Lacy, and Amethyst felt tears trickle down her own cheeks. She moved back, not wanting to be seen, but she stayed close enough to see Cobalt close his eyes, and whisper his consent to be called to Earth.

When he disappeared from view, Amethyst felt a dull ache in her heart, and then after a moment, it disappeared, and her tears stopped. She blinked a few times, but suddenly, the melancholy and weird feelings of having recognised Cobalt disappeared.

Confused, but also relieved, Amethyst left the Angelic Garden and went back to her room. She got into bed and once safe under the covers, she closed her eyes and drifted off into a peaceful sleep.

Mica was heading to Angelton when he crossed paths with the Professor of Patience.

"Oh, Miracle! I was going to speak with Velvet, but perhaps I may have a word with you instead?"

Mica nodded and gestured at a nearby bench in the Underwater Garden. They both sat, and Mica waited for the Old Soul to speak.

"In my class yesterday I watched an Angel looking after an Indigo Child. They came in together, sat together, and the Angel helped throughout the class. I then noticed that they left together for the next class."

Mica nodded, unsure where the Old Soul was going with the conversation.

"It occurred to me, after sitting in on your and Emergence's class on family connections, that perhaps what the Children need to thrive is a strong, secure connection to an adult. In this case, to the Earth Angel trainees. I was thinking that we could assign a Child to each trainee, and we could create families and communities. I think that the trainees would thrive on having souls to care for, and the Children would thrive with the guidance."

Mica sat back and considered her idea. It resonated deeply within him, and he knew that the Old Soul was right. Every child needed a secure, strong connection to an adult to feel safe and cared for. And if they created families at the Academy, perhaps they would remember their connections when on Earth, and not feel isolated or alone.

He nodded. "I think it's a brilliant idea. I will tell Emergence and Velvet, and see if we can start it soon, as I believe the Crystal Children will be arriving in the next year or so, and it would be good to have this programme already in effect before they arrive, to make sure it works."

Cotton smiled at him. "Wonderful. I do think it will help everyone involved. And who knows, perhaps those Children will actually be born to the trainees who have adopted them here."

"It is entirely possible. In which case, their connection would be even stronger. And souls with strong, healthy connections do tend to do amazing things with their lives."

"Yes, they do," Cotton agreed. "Thank you for listening and for taking my idea to Velvet. I must get back. My next class begins shortly."

"Thank you for all your wisdom and hard work, Cotton. We really appreciate it."

Cotton nodded and stood up. "Likewise, Oracle."

Mica watched her leave the garden, her long hair drifting about behind her in the invisible current. Her idea really was an excellent one. Especially now they knew the Indigos remembered their previous lives on Earth. It would be helpful for them to have some extra guidance and support. Instead of continuing on to Angelton to visit the bakery as planned, Mica decided to head back to his room to see if Emerald was there. They had another piece of the jigsaw puzzle to plan and put into action.

* * *

"Velvet, it's good to see you again, it has been far too long!"

The two Old Souls embraced, then sat on the floral sofa in the coffee shop. Velvet looked around.

"You seem to spend a lot of time in bars and coffee shops, or in purple tents. Really not where I would imagine you being."

Magenta chuckled. "I decided to try some new locations. But I must say, Fifth Dimension baristas aren't the best. I hope you find better ones when you get to Earth."

"Are you sure you are not coming? Even for the coffee?" Velvet was joking, but Magenta could see the seriousness of the question in her eyes.

"I feel I will be needed here. After all, who would Corduroy and Tartan consult if I were to leave?"

"Another Seer?" Velvet smiled. "You are not the only one in the dimension."

"True," Magenta said. "One of the very best is sat right next to me."

Velvet frowned. "What do you mean?"

Magenta sighed. "My dear Velvet. You are a Seer who has simply shut down her sight. You once taught me how to See."

"I did?" Velvet sat back on the sofa, a frown still on her face. "Why do I not remember? Or have visions now?"

"I think it's because you had one that scared you. So you shut them off. But if it wasn't for that scary vision, you wouldn't have saved all the lives that you did." Magenta felt a bit nervous bringing up Atlantis. After all, Emerald had warned her not to remind Velvet of anything that might bring up memories of Laguz. But they had both agreed that Velvet needed to See her new future for herself, so that she would finally step into her own power. Despite the great many advances during the past decade at the Academy, Magenta could see that her Old Soul friend was still not fully owning her own authority.

"I still don't remember."

"It doesn't matter. You don't need to remember the past in order to See the future."

"And you think I should try to See again? To open up what I have closed off?" Velvet sat up. "Wait a minute, are the déjà vu visions?"

Magenta shook her head. "No, they are memories from another timeline, that's different. But if you could See, for yourself and not just second-hand through me, exactly who you are destined to be, then I believe that the world would shift so much faster."

"How do I do it? How do I See?"

"I think water used to help you," Magenta said, again nervous that it would remind Velvet of the beach. "And you used to have vivid dreams."

Velvet sighed. "I don't dream here. When I rest, there is nothing. I will spend some time near the water. There is a wonderful waterfall in the Angelic Garden."

"That's perfect," Magenta said, relieved. "The sound of the water should help you to focus. And then set your intention to See yourself on Earth."

Velvet nodded. "Thank you, that's very helpful."

"You're welcome." Magenta sipped her bitter coffee and winced. "So what was it you came to see me about?" she asked.

"Oh!" Velvet said. "Yes, I had completely forgotten. I came to ask your opinion on a new idea that has arisen. For the Children to be adopted by trainees."

*　*　*

Aria was working in the Elemental Garden when she received the notice. She wiped her muddy hands on her t-shirt before taking the note from the messenger, and she opened it up, curious, as she never usually received mail.

She unfolded the lilac paper, and read it, her eyes growing bigger.

"A Child? They are giving me a Child?"

She read it again, more slowly this time, absorbing the words. They had begun the adoption programme months before, and she thought that perhaps she wasn't going to be assigned a Child, because she hadn't been given an Indigo. But Aria squealed in excitement as she read the note a second time. She was to adopt a Crystal Child, who would be assigned to her when they arrived in just a few weeks.

Too excited to continue working, Aria put her tools away, then ran to the bookshop, where Shelly was working, to tell her the news. She reached the shop, and burst through the door, startling a Starperson who was sitting quietly in an armchair in the corner reading a very large book with symbols all over the cover. Tracking mud all over the carpet but not caring, Aria ran through the maze of bookshelves, calling out Shelly's name.

She was on the third floor, and just turned the corner into the marine biology section when she finally saw her friend's red hair.

"Shelly!"

The Mermaid dropped the book she was holding and jumped at the sound of her voice being shouted. "Aria!" she said, shaking her head and leaning down to pick the book up. "You scared me, what's wrong?"

"Nothing! I just had some exciting news! I'm going to have a child!"

Shelly dropped the book again and her mouth fell open. "It's possible for that happen here?" she asked. Her shocked gaze dropped to Aria's stomach. "You're pregnant?"

Aria burst out laughing. "No, no, I'm not pregnant!" She held out the letter to her friend, who took it and skimmed the words.

"Oh, of course! I see," Shelly said. "That's wonderful." She handed the note back and Aria frowned. Her friend really didn't sound that excited for her.

"What's wrong? Don't you think I will be good at it? Do you think I'll mess them up somehow?"

Shelly shook her head and smiled. "Oh, Aria, I think you will be wonderful with them, that's not, I mean, um," she trailed off, and then picked up the book at her feet and busied herself with putting it away and tidying the shelf next to her.

"What is it then?"

Shelly sighed. "I haven't been told whether I will be assigned a Child. All of the Indigos have been adopted, and now they are assigning the Crystals. What if they don't ask me? I would, well, I would very much like to care for someone."

"Oh," Aria said, feeling a little deflated. "I'm sure they will ask you, maybe you will get a Rainbow, or even a Diamond! There are plenty more Children to come yet. I'm sure they won't forget you."

Shelly smiled, and her face brightened. "You are right, of course. I'm sorry to dampen your good news. I really am happy for you, you will be wonderful. And I look forward to meeting them."

Aria grinned, her energy lifting again. "Thank you, I will do my very best!"

The clock on the town square chimed and Aria's eyes widened. "Oops! I should go back to work. I kind of just left in the middle of the job."

Shelly laughed and shooed her out of the shop. "I'll see you later!" she called out as Aria ran back to the gardens.

*   *   *

"What will I do when you are called?"

Amethyst smiled at her Indigo Child, who was sitting next to her, cutting out a doll from the fabric scraps from Amethyst's dressmaking.

"You will continue your classes, and you will be well looked after. You could still hang out here. The other seamstresses won't mind."

"But I will miss you so much."

Amethyst put her scissors down and put her arm around the child. "My sweet Indigo. I will be with you always. Remember the star that Starlight gave you that resides within your heart chakra?"

The Child nodded and touched the centre of her chest.

"I am within that star also. So when you go within and connect to your star, you are connecting to me. We can never be separated, no matter what dimensions we are each in."

The Child smiled up at Amethyst. "I can feel you there."

"Good. Always remember that. You are never alone, ever."

"You are a beautiful Angel," the Child said quietly. "I am so thankful that they assigned me to you."

"Me too. I love you, and always will."

"I love you too." The Child wrapped her arms around Amethyst, and the Angel held her tightly.

Despite her words of reassurance and comfort, she too

was wary of the day she would be called to Earth, as she had grown accustomed to her life here, and had grown very fond of her Indigo Child. She didn't feel ready for it to be over yet. But she knew that it would soon be time, after all, the population at the Academy had been dwindling since the first trainee had been called quite some time ago.

Of course, she might be worrying for no reason. Many of the Indigo Children were also being called, and so her own may be called to Earth before her. In which case, it would be she who would need to go within to connect.

"I promised I would meet some of the Crystals in the Planetary Garden, may I finish this later?"

Amethyst smiled. "Of course, just put it in your box so it's safe."

The Child tidied away her fabric and thread, and then kissed Amethyst on the cheek before skipping out the door. Amethyst watched her go, feeling like she could burst with happiness, pride and love. If it felt like this to have children on Earth, she couldn't wait to have her own.

CHAPTER TWENTY

"You called, Velvet?" Starlight asked, stepping into the Old Soul's office.

"Yes, I wondered if you knew what to do?"

Starlight approached the large multifaceted crystal on Velvet's desk, and smiled. "It is the Rainbows. They are contained within this crystal. Simply hang it up in the sunlight, and they will appear."

Velvet looked at the clear crystal and frowned. "But won't they need to be in human form in order to fully participate in classes and activities? Not in light form?"

"I have already spoken to them about this," Starlight assured her. "When they appear as lights for the first time in the Academy, their forms will solidify into human bodies."

Velvet sighed in relief. "Oh, that's good, thank you. I will do so immediately." She smiled at Starlight. "Do you know when the Diamonds are arriving?"

"They will arrive in the next year or so. They are very excited to get here. They are truly the clearest, brightest and most pure souls I have ever met."

"I do hope that Earth does not dim their light," Velvet

said. "When are they likely to be called?"

"Oh, they will be here for a while yet. I think you will be leaving before they do."

Velvet nodded. "That's good, they will get plenty of preparation then. Shall we take the Rainbows to an empty room and greet them properly?"

Starlight nodded, and she waved her arm, causing herself, Velvet, and the crystal to reappear in classroom 334. Starlight waved her hand again, and the crystal moved up into the air, and began to slowly rotate. Velvet smiled and clicked her fingers. Sunlight streamed through the ceiling, hitting the clear crystal and filling the room with dancing rainbows of light.

Starlight reached out to catch one, and held it gently in her palm. "It is time," she said softly.

One by one, the rainbows morphed and changed, until they were fully formed, multi-coloured Children, standing in a circle. There were so many of them, Velvet was unable to do an accurate head count. But she knew there were at least a hundred.

"Welcome, Rainbows! Welcome to the Earth Angel Training Academy. I am Velvet, the Head of the Academy."

The Children bowed their heads in greeting, and a Child with piercing orange eyes and purple hair stepped forward. "Greetings, Velvet," he said. "We are happy to be here at the Academy, and look forward to learning what we need to thrive on Earth. We are not used to human bodies, so may we have a few days to adjust?"

"Of course! I will show you to your rooms, and then introduce you to the Earth Angels who will look after you. You may begin classes in a week, once you are used to the Academy and your bodies."

The Child smiled. "Thank you. We appreciate your understanding and support."

"As we appreciate yours. We know that you come from a very beautiful planet to help us with the situation on Earth, and we are very grateful," Velvet said with a smile. "Now, perhaps it would be best if we split you up into two groups, and maybe Starlight can show half of you to your rooms."

Velvet looked at the Angel of Destiny, who was already nodding. "Yes, of course I can, it would be my pleasure." She walked towards the door, and exactly half of the Children moved to follow her. When they had all filtered out, Velvet turned to her half and nodded for them to follow. The Children followed her out, and Velvet glanced back to see that with their colourful hair and clothing, they looked like a moving, rippling rainbow. She had a feeling that they would soon transform the world with their colours alone.

As they walked through the Academy, she could see them looking at the new colour scheme in the hallways with great interest. Velvet was beginning to get used to the Academy looking like the inside of a kaleidoscope, but for the first few weeks it had given her headaches.

She had to admit though, the rate of trainees and Children getting lost had reduced dramatically. And she felt better about leaving the Academy, knowing that the Angelton Council would keep things running smoothly, along with the professors who had chosen to stay behind. She had not chosen anyone in particular to run the Academy, but felt that a joint effort between the souls who remained would work well. And of course, the Oracles would oversee things until they too went to Earth.

She and Starlight spent the next hour ensuring all of the Rainbows found their rooms and understood where things were and how to ask for help. Then they asked the Rainbows to join them in the main hall later that day, where Starlight would gift them with their star. It made sense to do the ceremony immediately, so that no information would be lost.

When they were all settled, Velvet returned to her office for a brief rest while Starlight returned to the heavens to prepare for the ceremony.

Velvet relaxed into her chair and closed her eyes. She had been trying to See for some time now, ever since Magenta had told her that she was capable, but she had yet to See or sense anything except the odd salty breeze and a glimmer of sunlight on the waves. Certainly nothing coherent that would give her a better idea of what was to come in her next earthly life.

Wind chimes sounded and she sighed. There really was no time to rest these days. She opened her eyes and looked at the wall to her left. "Yes, Beryl?"

*   *   *

"So are there any other questions?"

The Root Chakra group looked up at Emerald and all of them shook their heads, except for one.

"Was there something you wanted to ask, Amethyst?"

The Angel smiled. "Yes, but it has nothing to do with the lesson."

Emerald chuckled. "Ask anyway, it might help anyone else who has the same query."

"I was wondering, well, when the Diamond Children arrive, will there be the opportunity for those of us whose Children have already been called to be able to adopt again?"

Emerald saw the sadness in the Angel's eyes and she sighed. "I believe that those who have yet to adopt a Child will have priority, and I am not sure how many Diamonds are coming," she said, not wanting to make any promises she couldn't keep. "When was your Child called? Indigo?"

Amethyst smiled. "Yes, she was an Indigo. She was called to Earth just a few days ago. I had believed that I would leave first, but it seems she was ready."

"I know you must miss her, but knowing that you created such a safe, nurturing space for her here, which will help her to connect and create secure attachments on Earth, must be a comfort?"

Amethyst looked down at her hands. "I do miss her. And I know she will be fine on Earth without me, but it was difficult to say goodbye."

Emerald's heart broke for the Angel, and she went over to her and crouched beside her. "Angel, there will be many more difficult moments in your life, and there will be much pain and sadness. But I do believe that if you focus on the happy moments, on the times that you had together, that you can get through this. And I promise," she said, patting her hand. "That if there is the opportunity for you to adopt again, I will certainly let you know."

Amethyst smiled at her, and nodded. "Thank you, Oracle. I am very grateful for your compassion and understanding."

Emerald nodded and went back to the front of the room, her heart heavy. "You will all either experience leaving your Child here, or saying goodbye to your Child if they go to Earth before you," she said, addressing the whole group. "It is not an easy thing to go through, but if you reach out to those in your communities, and you focus on the amazing things you experienced and created together, then you will get through it."

The souls in the group nodded. Emerald could see that many of them had already said goodbye to their Children by the look on their faces.

"And remember, no matter where you are, you will always be connected to them, as long as you remember to connect to the star within you, because they are there."

She smiled at Amethyst, who smiled back, a look of genuine joy on her face.

* * *

A mere eleven months after the quiet, unannounced arrival of the Rainbow Children, Starlight found herself back at the Academy, awaiting the arrival of the Diamonds. It seemed that the Faeries had gone all out in their bid to welcome the Diamonds, having been upset that they had missed out on the arrival of the Rainbows.

Starlight surveyed the main hall from the stage, and felt like she was at a carnival of some sort. There were lights and bunting and decorations of all colours everywhere, and every soul still remaining at the Academy had come. They had even set up a smaller stage and had a band playing.

Velvet was pacing back and forth a bit nervously, and Emerald and Mica were talking quietly between themselves. Starlight closed her eyes briefly to tune into the Diamonds, and sensed that they were near. She looked over to Velvet who caught her eye, and she nodded.

Velvet nodded back and turned to address the party below them. "Earth Angels and Children! I believe that the Diamonds will be with us very shortly, if we could please reduce the noise level, so we don't scare them?"

The band stopped playing, and the excited chattering lowered to an excited whispering. Velvet looked back at Starlight who nodded again. She could feel them getting closer and closer, and in fact...

She reached out to grab her sister's arm and tugged her to the side of the stage, and the Oracles, obviously sensing the Diamonds too, did the same.

Moments later, about seventy beams of light shone down like lasers onto the centre of the stage. The crowd hushed and stared at the stage in silent anticipation.

Starlight watched as the most stunning, completely clear, faceted diamonds appeared within the beams, moving downward until they hovered just above the floor. The beams then collapsed into the diamonds, and when they merged, mini supernovas were created briefly, making Starlight blink and look away for a moment.

When she looked back, a group of Children, whose skin shone and glimmered, like their namesake, stood in a diamond formation.

After a moment, the crowd burst into applause, and far from being scared, the Diamonds smiled, and then bowed to the crowd.

Velvet allowed the applause and cheers to go on for a minute, then she stepped forward to greet the new Children.

"My dear Diamonds, we are most thrilled to welcome you to the Earth Angel Training Academy. I hope your journey here was uneventful?"

The tallest Diamond stepped forward to shake her hand, catching her slightly by surprise. "We are most excited to be here too, Velvet. We shall do what we can to help Earth and her people. What is the first thing we must do?"

Starlight could see that Velvet was a little taken aback so she stepped forward. "I shall be gifting you each with a star, so that you remember your training here at the Academy, and so that you remember who you truly are once you get to Earth. And then," she said with a smile, waving her arm at the crowd. "We shall celebrate."

The Diamond Child smiled at Starlight and nodded. "That sounds perfect."

While the Earth Angel trainees and the other Children chattered amongst themselves, Starlight performed the Star Ceremony with the new Diamonds. When she had finished and was just about to leave, Mica reached out to her and touched her arm.

"Stay and celebrate," he said with a smile. "We would never have got to this point without you."

Starlight smiled. "I guess I could stay for a short while."

She didn't resist when Velvet pulled her towards the band, and started dancing. She couldn't remember the last time she had just relaxed and moved to music, and wasn't thinking about the next thing she had to do.

As she twirled under the fairy lights, and saw the Diamond Children joining in with the celebrations, she smiled and allowed herself to let go.

CHAPTER TWENTY-ONE

Emerald was in her and Mica's room, surveying the now three walls filled with notes, after having been at the Academy for just over twenty years.

She couldn't quite believe that they had managed to achieve so much. She looked at their notes on the Children, the adoption programme, Angelton, the elections (of which there had now been many, giving each party chance to experience running the town, although it seemed as though the Faeries had had a winning streak for several years.) The Academy had also gained something of a reputation, and was attracting more Earth Angel trainees from other schools and Academies in the Fifth Dimension, and also from other dimensions. So they'd had no shortage of trainees to teach.

Emerald smiled as she thought of all the celebrations they'd had, when trainees were called to Earth. A larger bell had been installed in the town square, and it was a well-known phrase, that every time the bell rang, another Earth Angel gained their earth wings.

She studied their notes on their discussions with the Starpeople, detailing the ways that they could use their advanced technology to create communities, and to ensure that good health came before profit. The Starpeople had relished the challenge, and many had already been called to Earth, hopefully to begin sowing the seeds of a community driven society.

If she hadn't already seen the visions of the new Earth, Emerald would have struggled to imagine a world where the vast number of people weren't glued to a screen of some kind. She knew that in the new world, they'd spend more time connecting to others in person, rather than through social media.

Emerald was pleased and amazed at the number of businesses and organisations the Earth Angels had created too. They had grasped the importance of entrepreneurship and leadership, as well as finances and politics. They had run successful businesses, raised funds to save animals and forests and the sea. Of course, it was all theoretical here, as there was no one that needed saving in the Fifth Dimension, but Emerald was convinced that these skills would prove incredibly useful when they got to Earth.

Despite her initial resistance to returning to Earth, for fear of losing Mica, Emerald had to admit that excitement was building up within her, and she couldn't wait to see and experience this new world for herself. She had a feeling it was going to be truly magical.

She noticed the time and realised she was going to be late for her meeting with Magenta. She closed her eyes, and when she opened them, she was opposite the Old Soul in deep pink robes in a coffee shop overlooking the ocean.

"My apologies, Magenta, I was absorbed in my work," she said, as she sat down in the empty chair.

Magenta looked up from where she had been gazing

into space and smiled. "No fear, you are perfectly on time." She picked up her cup and sipped her drink, then winced. "No matter how much I complain, they still are incapable of producing a decent cup of coffee."

Emerald chuckled. "Nothing quite matches the coffee on Earth, does it? What can I do for you? You said it was urgent that we meet."

Magenta set her cup down and sighed. "I have been receiving visions of myself on Earth again."

Emerald's eyes widened. "Oh, that's interesting. How do you feel about that?"

"I want to hate the idea, as I had decided to leave here and find my Flame in the higher dimensions after Velvet had left for Earth... but the visions are rather glorious, and I find myself curious about this new world you are creating."

"We," Emerald said. "The world *we* are creating. If it weren't for you, we wouldn't be doing any of this."

Magenta chuckled. "I forget that I was the one who started all of this. I wish I could remember."

"My memories of the second timeline have very much faded now," Emerald admitted. "There are only a few things that really stand out: happy memories of the woods, chocolate cake, and laughter around a camp fire."

"Are you and Mica still returning? Or have you changed your mind?"

"We are returning. I have had my doubts, but, like you, I am curious. And in fact, with all of the celebrations that have occurred, I am actually excited. I am also certain Mica and I will find each other because we have decided to return as walk-ins."

"Oh, that's a good idea. None of that having to grow up nonsense."

Emerald chuckled. "Indeed. And if we step into older bodies, we will be able to help immediately, and we won't have to stay for too long. Then we can return home and spend all of eternity in the Angelic Realm together."

"You deserve to retire," Magenta joked. "You have been in service long enough."

"Indeed," Emerald agreed. She picked up the cup in front of her and drank some of the brown liquid, then nearly choked. "I see what you mean," she said, patting her mouth with a napkin. "That's even worse than Mica's famous hangover cure."

Magenta laughed. "I know where we can get a better drink." She clicked her fingers and the two of them were now seated at a bar.

"Now this is more like it," Emerald said with a smile. "Can I have a cherry and an umbrella in mine?"

When they both had a colourful drink in their hands, Magenta held hers up. "To returning to Earth, and experiencing the Diamond Age."

Emerald clinked her glass with Magenta's and nodded. "To the Diamond Age."

*   *   *

"Loser!"

Tom's shoulders hunched up and his head bowed low. He walked past the group of boys quickly, trying to pretend he couldn't hear their taunts. He had told his mum he shouldn't take the Star Trek lunchbox to school. She had insisted he take it because it was his favourite, but the other kids thought he was a freak for liking a TV show about spaceships.

He couldn't explain why he loved it so much, it just felt so familiar to him. He went into the classroom early, and sat at the back of the room. He took out his sandwich and ate it slowly, hoping he wouldn't get in trouble for eating inside. He just couldn't sit outside with the other kids. They were too mean to him.

"Hello, Tom."

Tom looked up to see his teacher at her desk. He flushed red and looked down at his lunch. He could hear her approach him, but he didn't look up. It was only when she was crouched next to him, her face level with his, that he dared look up to meet her eye. This close, he could see that her eyes were really odd. There was a lighter ring of colour around her pupils.

"Are you okay?" she asked softly. "Didn't you want to play outside with the others?"

Tom shook his head. "I prefer being on my own."

His teacher smiled. "I can understand that. I feel the same way sometimes. Have you written anymore stories lately? I loved the one you wrote about the angels."

Tom smiled. "I haven't, but I had some new ideas for one."

His teacher nodded. "I look forward to reading it. You are a very good writer, Tom." She stood up and went back to her desk, and this time Tom's cheeks were flushed red with pride.

She liked his stories. Thought he was a good writer. He couldn't wait to tell his mum.

At the end of the day, Tom was still riding high on his teacher's praise, when he stepped out into the playground and a hand reached out and grabbed his lunchbox, throwing it to the ground. It burst open and the empty wrappers from his lunch scattered everywhere. He saw the boys laughing, and he felt anger rise up inside.

"Nerd!"

"Loser!"

Tom bent down to pick up the rubbish, his heart pounding furiously. Someone's shoe came into contact with his backside and he pitched forward, hitting the gravel with his chin. He lay on the ground while the children laughed, and tears welled up in his eyes. In that moment, all he wanted was to go home. He didn't belong here.

He scrunched his eyes closed, and clutched his chest, and wished as hard as he could to just disappear into himself.

A moment passed and the laughter receded, and everything went quiet. Tom could see a bright light, and hoped that it was going to take him away from this place. He went towards the light until he was engulfed in it, and it turned into a large screen. He watched as images flew across it, and suddenly he understood.

He knew who he was. He knew where he had come from. And he knew why he was here.

His eyes flew open, and he lay still for a moment, trying to absorb everything he had just remembered. Out of nowhere, a large white feather drifted down and landed next to him, just inches away from his face. He smiled, and then started laughing. Out of the corner of his eye he could see the group of boys backing away from him. Still chuckling, he stood up, wiped the gravel and blood from his chin, dusted himself down and then looked around at the group of boys who were backing further away, with something more like fear than derision on their faces.

He gave them a little nod, picked up his lunchbox, and then walked confidently towards the gate where his mother was waiting.

"Oh, Tom! Oh my goodness! What happened to you?"

His mother gathered him up in her arms, and he breathed in her scent. He smiled at her and shrugged. "I just tripped."

"Oh, and you dented your lunchbox! Let's get you home and get you cleaned up."

Tom nodded, and then blinked as he saw a pair of wings behind his mother, made from the purest white light. "You are an angel," he said in awe.

His mother laughed. "Thank you, and you are my little Starperson from the Fifth Dimension."

Tom's eyes widened. He had forgotten that she sometimes called him that. He knew now that she was right. Because that's who he was. He was Tm of Zubenelgenubi. A Starperson. From the Fifth Dimension.

And now that he had remembered, he would never forget.

* * *

"Wow! What's that?"

Aria followed Shelly's gaze to the sky above Angelton and her eyes widened. "Wow, that's beautiful! Has it been there the whole time?"

Shelly shook her head. "No, I swear it just appeared."

The two Earth Angels gazed up at the bright star that now shone above their town.

"Hey, do you know where the star came from?" Rosa asked them as she was passing by.

"No, we don't," Aria replied. "I wonder if-" she broke off her sentence with a gasp as two more stars shot across the sky, stopping next to the first one, glowing brightly.

"Oh my goodness," she breathed. "You don't think…"

Shelly looked at her. "Think what?"

"The stars within. Do you think these stars mean that Earth Angels are remembering? That they are connecting to the star within?"

Shelly smiled and looked up at the three stars. "I think you could be right! Shall we tell Velvet? Or the Oracles? Oh this is so exciting!"

Aria nodded and the two of them left the crowd that had now gathered to stare in awe at the bright lights, and made their way to Velvet's office. They knocked and waited to be admitted.

"How can I help you?" Velvet asked, glancing up at them as they entered.

"We think it's working!" Aria squeaked, her excitement getting the better of her.

Velvet frowned. "What is working?"

"Come with us," Shelly urged. "We will show you."

Velvet still looked confused, but complied with their request. They called upon the Oracles on the way, and soon they joined the crowd, staring up at the lights above Angelton. There were now five.

"Does this mean…" Velvet whispered.

"Yes," Emergence replied. "The Earth Angels are waking up, and finding the star within."

Aria looked up at the Oracle, and saw tears in her eyes. "I knew that was what it meant!" she said. She looked back at the stars. "I wonder if one of them is Tim."

"I would think so," Shelly said.

Aria smiled. She heard her name and she turned to Velvet. "Yes?"

Velvet frowned. "What?"

"You just said my name?" Aria asked.

Velvet shook her head. "No, I didn't say anything. No one said anything." Her eyes widened. "Did you just hear someone calling you?"

Aria nodded. "Oh! Is it the Angels?" she heard it again and she jumped. "It is! Oh my goodness! They're calling me to Earth!" Excitement flooded through her and she ran over to the bell in the middle of the square, and rang it. "I've been called! I'm going to Earth! I'm getting my Earth Angel wings!"

Cheers erupted all around her, and out of the crowd, her Child, Garnet, came running over to hug her. Someone started playing music, and lights appeared, and as had happened many times over the years since Tm left, a party broke out.

Aria was hugged and kissed over and over by her fellow trainees and the Children, and she laughed and twirled about the dancefloor, excited to be going to Earth, especially now that she knew that the stars within worked, and that she would remember everything.

A short while later, the call was getting louder and she found herself standing in front of her very best friend, Shelly.

"Promise me you won't forget me. That you will find me. I hope I get called soon so I can see you there," Shelly said over the music and laughter.

Aria's eyes welled up. "I will miss you, Mermaid. We have achieved so much together!"

Shelly threw her arms around the smaller soul. "I will miss you too! And yes we have. But how exciting! You will go to Earth and start Awakening people. And save the whales and the oceans!"

Aria grinned at all the exclamations. "Yes, I will. And when you get there and we find each other, we will start our organisation, and we will save the animals for real, not just in theory."

"Sisters forever?" Shelly asked.

"Sisters forever," Aria confirmed.

"I will see you there."

"See you there!" Aria said, giving her friend one more hug before closing her eyes and answering the call.

CHAPTER TWENTY-TWO

"Are you alright, my dear Crystal?"

The Child looked up at Amethyst. "I have torn my dress. And my Earth Angel was just called to Earth, so I cannot ask her to fix it for me."

Tears filled the Child's eyes and spilled over. Amethyst knelt to the floor and pulled her into her arms. "My sweet Child, it's okay, I can fix that for you. It just needs a few stitches. Come, sit down and I will do it for you."

"Thank you," the Child whispered, taking the seat she was offered.

Amethyst got her sewing needle and selected some matching thread, then sat next to the Child and began to sew the torn hem. "What was your Earth Angel's name, little one?"

"Aria. She was a Faerie."

Amethyst smiled. She had heard of the green Faerie called Aria. She had created quite a buzz at the Academy, but Amethyst had not really had a chance to speak with her much. "I bet that was fun, having a Faerie care for you."

The Child smiled. "It was a lot of fun, and she really did

care for me. She was upset when she said goodbye, but she was so excited to go to Earth."

"I bet she was, are you excited too?" Amethyst asked, carefully stitching the tear. The Child nodded. "What is your name?"

"Garnet," the Child replied.

"Well, Garnet, would you like to learn how to sew? My Child was an Indigo, and she was called to Earth some time ago. She was making a doll before she left. It seems a shame to leave it half finished."

Garnet's eyes lit up and she smiled. "I think I might enjoy that very much," she said shyly.

Amethyst smiled at the Child and finished mending her dress. She trimmed the thread and Garnet grinned. "Thank you, Angel, I am very thankful."

Amethyst got up and went to the back room, and picked up the box containing the half-finished doll and the clothing her Indigo Child had been making.

"Here," she said, coming out to the front where Garnet still sat. "I will show you some stitches, and then you could finish this if you wanted."

Not caring that she had lots of clothes to make, and classes in the afternoon, Amethyst sat and patiently showed Garnet how to sew. She felt lighter than she had in a long time.

*   *   *

"I'm so sorry, Leon," Velvet said to the Faerie.

"Don't apologise. You have suppressed your Sight for a long time, it makes sense that it would take a long time to return," the grey Faerie Seer reassured her.

"But I've been trying to See for over a decade now. I really don't think it's coming back."

"Let's give it one more go?"

Velvet sighed and nodded. She stared at the waterfall and let her vision glaze over until the falling sparkling water was like a shimmering blur in front of her. She concentrated on the sound of the water hitting the smooth rocks, and set her intention to See the future.

Suddenly she was standing behind a podium, making a speech about human rights. There were flashes of light all around her, but that didn't stop her from passionately making her point to the crowd assembled. She felt a burning feeling in the centre of her chest, and her shoulders straightened and she suddenly felt like she had a large pair of feathered wings unfurling from her back and spreading out either side of her.

Every word she uttered was charged with authority and power, and she knew that she was making a difference. She was making history. She was Awakening the world.

Velvet blinked and found herself sitting on the golden bench in the Angelic Realm with Leon sat next to her. She turned to the Faerie, a fire in her eyes. "I saw it. I saw myself in a position of authority. I saw myself making a difference."

Leon grinned. "I knew it! I knew you would See today!"

Velvet frowned. "How did you know?"

"Because I have been called. But there was something inside that told me I wouldn't leave until my mission here was complete."

Velvet threw her arms around him and hugged him. "Oh, that's wonderful! I am so excited for you! Thank you for not giving up on me. You have been so very patient over these last few years. I know I was losing faith that I would

See."

"Of course. I always knew you would get there. But now I must leave." Leon winced. "It is getting too loud to ignore now."

"Much love to you, Faerie. I wish you a happy and successful human life."

"Thank you, Velvet. You too."

Velvet watched the Faerie walk away towards the town square, presumably to ring the bell and celebrate his new adventure with everyone. She understood now, that her role on Earth would be a powerful one. And that despite her initial reservations about leaving her Academy to become human for the 3333rd time, she knew without a shred of doubt, that she was needed there. She sat up straight, remembering the feeling of her ethereal wings unfurling and extending out, and she smiled. The Angels would be with her every step of the way. All she had to do was to connect to her star within and step into her true power.

With that empowering thought, all of her remaining feelings of self-doubt slipped away, and Velvet knew that it would all work out.

* * *

"Um, could you run that by me one more time?" Gold looked around the room full of Elders in confusion.

Silver sighed. "We have discussed the matter, and we think that you should return to Earth. Platinum will take over your post in the mists. The Earth is about to experience the most glorious age, and we think you should be there to experience it."

"Why me?" Gold asked, his eye twitching uncontrollably.

"Why not Copper? Or you? Or even Plutonium?"

Silver glanced around at the other Elders, then looked Gold in the eyes. "Because you are the strongest of us all. You have stood in the mists greeting souls for millennia. And it has never broken you. You have taken on all the pain, despair and heartbreak those souls bring home, and you have never faltered. We have been too sheltered here. We would never make it on Earth. But you would. You are strong, you are fearless. And the world needs you."

Gold shook his head. "You are wrong. It *does* break me. I *do* have fears. I am not infallible."

Silver smiled. "You are also humble. And honest. And that is the mark of a courageous soul."

Gold sighed. "Do I have a choice?"

"Of course. You have free will as much as any other soul. But please consider it."

Gold nodded. "I will let you know what I decide." He stood up, feeling shocked and unsettled. The other Elders bowed their heads to him as he left the room. He walked slowly down the path towards the mists, and called out in his mind for his love. When he reached his post where Opalite was standing, he saw Starlight was waiting there with her.

"You called, Gold? Are you okay?"

Gold nodded his thanks to Opalite who took the hint and flew back to the Angelic Realm. Gold looked into Starlight's eyes and sighed. "They wish for me to return to Earth," he said.

"The Oracles?" Starlight asked in surprise.

Gold shook his head. "No, the Elders. They said it's up to me, but, I feel I don't have a choice."

"Do you want to go? It's been so long..."

"I don't know. Maybe. But," he reached out and took her hand. "I don't wish to be away from you. So, I have a question."

After a long pause, Starlight chuckled nervously. "Yes?"

"Will you come with me? To Earth?"

"Oh." Starlight frowned and appeared to think for a few moments. "I wasn't expecting that."

Gold's heart sank. "I won't force you to accompany me, I just thought I would see..."

"Of course I will go," Starlight said, without hesitation.

Gold gripped her hand tighter. "Are you certain?"

Starlight smiled. "Yes. Once I am no longer needed here, I will follow you. I promise."

Gold pulled her into his arms, and embraced her hard, his hands gripping the feathers of her star-lit wings. "Thank you, my love. I know it won't be easy, but it will be much better if we are doing it together."

"It would be incredibly boring up here without you. Besides, I am keen to experience the Diamond Age for myself."

"Yes, as much as I resisted the Oracles' presence at first, and all the many, many changes, I have already been seeing changes on Earth, thanks to their teachings, and so I am also curious to see how it all works out."

Starlight kissed him lightly on the lips. "I must go, but I will visit again soon before we leave."

"Please do," Gold said. His attention was being pulled by the soul who was approaching through the mists. Before he could say anything, Starlight disappeared, leaving a little swirl of stars behind.

Gold breathed in deeply and brought his attention to the soul who had just crossed over and was in need of his counsel. It was odd, but he actually felt a glimmer of excitement too, at the idea of going to Earth. He hoped that was a good omen.

CHAPTER TWENTY-THREE

"Can you even believe the time is slipping by so quickly?" Emerald asked Mica, as they relaxed after yet another election. The Crystal Party had won this time. The Children were fast learners, and Emerald had no doubt that they would be running the place after Velvet was called.

Mica shook his head. "Thirty-four years. It's quite incredible. And to think – you were so impatient to get started when we arrived, so worried there wouldn't be enough time. But look at all that has occurred. It's amazing."

"It still doesn't feel like enough time, but I can feel that the time is coming closer for us to return to Earth."

"I can feel it too. Our presence here is becoming less and less needed, we have passed on as much information as we can. Now with the trainees teaching the new Earth Angels our lessons, we will not be missed when we do go."

"I think Velvet is ready too," Emerald said, sliding under the covers of their bed. "I can see that she is ready to go to Earth and fully step into her power. She has been different since she Saw it for herself. Far surer of herself."

"Do you think the original vision we Saw will fully

come to pass? Do you think she will remember, and become as influential as we have Seen?" Mica asked as he removed his robes and joined his Flame.

"Yes, I do. All she needs to do is to connect to her star within and the rest, as they say, is history."

"Or future," Mica said with a laugh.

Emerald giggled too. "I just feel so relieved that it all worked out. Judging by the number of stars above Angelton, a great number of the Earth Angels and Children have already Awoken, and that brings me so much joy."

"Me too. We did well, my love. We did well."

Emerald kissed him. "Yes, we did."

Mica yawned. "Let's get some rest." He kissed her back. "Goodnight, Emerald."

"Goodnight, Mica."

* * *

"So, are there any questions?"

Tom looked around the room, and set down the book that he had just done a reading from. At the age of twenty-four, he was already a published author. He was very popular in the Sci-Fi community, who loved his stories of other planets and angels and other beings.

"I have a question."

Tom nodded to the man. "Yes?"

"You write a lot about Faeries, and I wondered if you had ever actually encountered any? In real life?"

Tom smiled at the man. "What was your name?"

"Mike."

"Well, Mike, I'm sure many people would think me crazy, but yes, I have had encounters with Faeries in real life."

Mike smiled and nodded, as though it had confirmed something for him. "Thanks, I love your books, they're great."

"Thank you, Mike. Any other questions?"

"When are you going to write about the small green Faerie called Aria?"

Tom's eyes widened and his heart stopped. He sought out the source of the voice, and a blonde girl stood up, a grin on her face. "Aria?" he whispered.

"Hi, Tim."

"His name is Tom," a fan corrected her. Tom ignored him.

"Does anyone else have any questions?" Tom's agent asked the crowd when the silence stretched out too long.

Someone asked whether he was going to write a sequel, and Tom did his best to answer, but his mind was whirling. Despite remembering everything about his previous existence, he had yet to meet anyone he knew from the Academy. And he had never mentioned Aria in his books. How else would she know that if she wasn't actually her?

Once his agent finally let him go, Tom made a beeline for the girl.

"Aria?"

She looked up at him and grinned again. "Oh, Tim, you look exactly the same! I recognised you straight away from the picture in your book. And from you stories! When did you wake up and remember?" She tapped her hand to her chest and he shook his head in wonder.

"I was ten when I remembered everything."

"Oh, how cool! I was seven. Isn't it amazing? I remember it all!"

"Can we go somewhere?" Tom asked, aware that people were eavesdropping on their conversation.

"Sure. My mum is picking me up at three, so I have until then."

"How old are you?" Tom asked as they left the bookshop and headed to a coffee shop across the street.

"I'm fourteen," Aria replied. "And my human name is Arielle."

"Fourteen? You seem so much older," Tom commented. They ordered drinks then sat down and Aria smiled at him.

"That's because I am older. I was a Faerie for a very long time before being at the Academy for twenty years then coming here. But anyway, the reason I came to your book signing today is because you asked me to do something for you and I promised I would." Aria reached into her wallet and pulled out a worn piece of paper, its folds softened with age. "And here is my promise kept."

Tom frowned and took the paper. "I did? I don't think I remember that."

"You were waiting for a message when you left. It arrived seven years later. As soon as I connected to my star and everything came back to me I wrote down the message, because I was afraid I might forget." She laughed. "My short term memory is still pretty bad."

Tom's heart hammered as he looked down at the paper, and suddenly remembered the favour he had asked of the Faerie, so very long ago. "Au?" he whispered.

Aria nodded. "Read it."

His hands shaking, he unfolded the paper carefully, afraid of tearing it. In a childish but neat scrawl were the words sent through the galaxy from his dearest friend.

"Tm, I received your long-awaited message, and I

understand that this might not reach you before you are called to Earth, but in case it does, I want you to know that I am in awe of you. What you are doing is so very brave, and I know now that you are doing it for me. I hope you can forgive me for being upset. I love you, Au."

Tears streamed down Tom's face, and he didn't care who saw him cry. He looked up at Aria and shakily refolded the paper, placing it carefully in his own wallet. "Thank you," he whispered.

Aria smiled, tears spilling down her cheeks too. "You're welcome, Alien," she said, patting his hand. She reached into her pocket and handed him a blue handkerchief, and he took it with a chuckle, and wiped his eyes.

A bell rang then, as a barista was signalling that an order was ready to be served. Aria looked at Tom and giggled. "Do you remember?"

Tom blinked. "Yes! Of course, every time a bell rings-"

"Another Earth Angel gets their wings," Aria finished with a grin. "I'm so glad I started that! It was so much fun having a party every time an Earth Angel was called. Oh," she said, pulling out another piece of paper from her wallet. "I also did this for you."

He unfolded the paper, this one less creased and worn. "This is us?" he asked, studying the drawing.

Aria nodded. "Yes it is! In the room we shared in the Academy. You turned it into a galaxy, remember?"

Tm looked at the colourful drawing again and nodded. He wiped his eyes with his sleeve, his energy already feeling lighter. "Yes, I do remember. Thank you."

Aria grinned. "Anytime. I like drawing. So, when do I get my own book series then? I'll illustrate it."

Tom laughed, and said a silent thank you tor the

Universe for bringing the crazy Faerie back into his life. "I will see what I can do."

* * *

"It is time."

Corduroy looked up at Velvet from where he sat on the bench in the Atlantis Garden. "Are you ready?" he asked softly.

Velvet sat next to him, a whole array of emotions flitting in and out of her body, the overriding one being of excitement. "Yes, I am. And I must admit, I am excited to see how everything unfolds." She smiled at her friend. "It is not something I ever imagined I would have to do again, but I feel so grateful to have the chance." She looked around the garden. "I will miss this place though, it's so beautiful."

"It is," Corduroy agreed.

"And the souls I love are here," Velvet said, looking at him. He met her gaze, but his smile didn't reach his eyes.

"We will still be here when you get back."

"You don't think you might move on? Go on new adventures? I never got the impression you enjoyed being at the Academy much."

Corduroy chuckled. "I might do. Though I must say I've quite enjoyed the last few decades. Things got much more interesting when the Oracles arrived."

"Yes they did. It's hard to imagine what the Academy used to be like before," Velvet mused. The call from the Angels came again, louder than the last time. Velvet sighed.

"They are calling," Corduroy said.

"Yes." Velvet reached out to squeeze his leg through his heavy brown robes. "It has been a pleasure working with you here at the Academy, Corduroy. And I look forward to the day we meet again."

He nodded and patted her hand. He looked as though he was about to say something else, but then changed his mind. "Best of luck to you, Velvet."

She nodded and leaned forward to kiss her friend on the cheek. He closed his eyes and smiled. She clicked her fingers and left him there, sitting in front of the dolphin statue.

She reappeared in her office where the Oracles were waiting for her.

"Emergence, Miracle, what can I say? Words cannot effectively express how thankful I am to the both of you. For coming to help us, for everything you have taught the trainees, and for, well, saving the world from an untimely demise."

The Oracles glanced at one another and Emergence stepped forward to embrace the Old Soul.

"It was our pleasure, as well as our duty to help. We thank you for being so open to the changes, and for being willing to give up so much to make it a better world for everyone else."

Velvet smiled and embraced Miracle as well. "Will you remain here?"

"Only until the Diamonds are called forth. Then we will join you on Earth."

Velvet nodded and glanced around the room. She had already bid farewell to her close friends, and both Magenta and Beryl had already answered the call a few months ago. All that was left was to address the Children and trainees who had yet to be called. Though it felt wrong to leave before the Academy was empty, she was being called now and there was no way she could resist, even if she had wanted to. Besides, the Oracles would take care of everything in her stead. Along with Athena and Corduroy.

"They are waiting," Miracle said quietly.

Velvet glanced around the room then nodded at them. She knew she would miss this space, but felt comforted that the memory of it would remain within her. She clicked her fingers and the three of them appeared on the stage of the main hall, bringing the hushed chattering to silence.

She smiled at the small crowd of souls, who were mostly Crystal, Rainbow and Diamond Children, with a few Earth Angel trainees still scattered amongst them.

"My dear souls, it is time that I make my journey to Earth, and leave you in the very good care of the Oracles. I have so very much enjoyed working and living and learning with you all, and I look forward to the day that we meet on Earth." She breathed in deeply, and smiled brightly at them. She was so proud of them all. Something suddenly occurred to her. "When we do meet on Earth, if I have not yet connected to my star within, and I have not yet Awakened, then please help to wake me up."

She saw a few of the Children nod.

"Goodbye, everyone, I love you all and am so very proud of you," she said, backing away from the front of the stage. She was surprised when a number of the souls began to clap, and suddenly a wave of cheers and applause rippled through the room. Tears of joy streamed openly down her cheeks, and she bowed her head. "Thank you," she whispered, before leaving the stage and going out the side door. She was still composing herself when Emergence stepped through the door, looking for her.

"Peace, love and light be with you always," she

whispered, hugging the Old Soul one more time. "Save me some chocolate cake, okay?"

Velvet laughed through her tears and nodded. "I will. Thank you."

The call came again, making Velvet wince.

"Goodbye, Velvet."

"Goodbye, Emergence."

Velvet took a deep breath, then closed her eyes and whispered. "I'm ready."

*   *   *

"I guess we really don't need any of this anymore," Emerald said, looking at their notes, now covering every available space in their room.

Mica nodded. "I guess not. We have made all the changes we possibly can, it's all out of our hands now."

"What a relief," Emerald said, sitting heavily on the bed. "I still cannot believe that we managed to be here for so long without Velvet finding out the truth. And without her remembering her Flame."

Mica joined her on the bed and wrapped his arm around her waist. "I know. There were so many close moments, so many times when I thought it was all over and it would all be for nothing. But we made it. Velvet has gone to Earth, the Diamonds will follow in the next decade or so, and then we will follow them."

Emerald smiled at him. "As long as we find suitable souls."

Mica nodded. "Of course. We will wait until it is the right time."

Emerald looked at the walls. "Shall we burn it? It's

been a long time since we had a campfire. We could have a celebration in the town square."

"You know we could just make it all disappear?" Mica said.

"Of course, but where's the fun in that?" Emerald got up and started pulling the notes and diagrams and sketches from the walls, and placing them in a large bag.

Mica followed suit, and together they filled four bags with their plans. "Shall I put a notice out?"

Emerald nodded. "Yes, I think everyone deserves a break this evening. It's been a big day. Let's get the fire going first though, before you tell everyone to come."

Mica took two of the bags and Emerald took the other two, and they reappeared in the town square. Mica clicked his fingers to create a fire pit in the centre, then clicked his fingers again to create a fire.

"What a lazy way to start a fire," Corduroy commented as he walked by.

Mica chuckled. "True. I'm not setting a very good example am I?"

Corduroy settled on a bench nearby and watched the flames. "No, not really. So what is the occasion?"

"We thought we could have a campfire in honour of Velvet."

"And burn all your tax paperwork?" Corduroy joked, pointing at the bags.

Emerald laughed. "No, these were our notes for our classes. We figured that now Velvet had gone to Earth, we no longer needed them."

"I'm kind of surprised Oracles needed notes, isn't it all just up here?" Corduroy waved his hand at his head.

"We may be Oracles, but we are not infallible with

perfect recall," Mica said, emptying one of the bags onto the fire, making it flare up. "And there was much we needed to impart. We didn't want to forget anything."

Corduroy nodded. "It is an impressive amount that you have taught the trainees in a short amount of time, I will give you that."

Emerald smiled. "We appreciate your assistance, and your word."

Corduroy smiled. "I still don't fully understand it all, but I am a man of my word."

Mica nodded. "Yes you are. You are a good man, Corduroy."

"I wouldn't go that far," the Old Soul said darkly. He stood up. "I will leave you to the festivities."

"You won't join us?" Emerald asked. "We are inviting everyone."

"I'm not much into celebrating, and besides, I have lost a good friend today. I think I might just spend the evening in the Gardens."

Emerald walked around the fire and reached out to hug the Professor of Death. Mica could see he was resisting at first, but after a moment, he melted into Emerald's embrace.

"See you tomorrow," Mica said as the professor left the square. He met Emerald's gaze. "I Ic'll be okay," he reassured her.

Emerald nodded, but the tears in her eyes glittered in the flame light. "I know."

The celebration went on well into the night, with the glittering stars lighting up the sky above them. Mica watched Emerald dancing around the campfire with a Diamond Child and a Crystal Child, and he smiled. A deep feeling of peace washed over him, and he gave a silent thanks to the

Universe, for helping him and his Flame change the fate of the planet called Earth, and all of her inhabitants. He was excited to experience the new age that they had created, and to live the life of an Awakened Earth Angel.

It would be the best adventure yet.

CHAPTER TWENTY-FOUR

The Other Side. Eighty-four years later.

"Welcome home, Velvet."

Velvet stepped through the mists, and was surprised to see two of her dearest old friends, Gold and Starlight waiting for her. "What are you doing here?" she asked, hugging them both in turn. "Though it's so good to see you, I thought you would be at home in the stars."

"We were," Starlight said with a smile. "But we couldn't miss your homecoming."

Velvet smiled at the Angel of Destiny. "I am honoured. Have you come to take me back to the stars with you?"

"You don't want me to ask the question?" Gold said, his eye twitching.

Velvet chuckled. "No, thank you. The Diamond Age far surpassed all of my expectations, and I have to say, it was the best human life of my existence. But I think eighty-four years was plenty long enough. It's time to go home now."

"It truly was magnificent, wasn't it?" Starlight mused.

"Yes, it was. And I'm so pleased that we got to experience

it together," Velvet said. "So, shall we?"

Starlight and Gold glanced at each other. "I'm afraid you cannot come home with us," Starlight said.

Velvet frowned. "What? Why not?"

"Because there is somewhere else you need to be," Gold said. He glanced behind him and Velvet saw a figure approaching them through the mists.

"Greetings, Velvet, welcome back."

"Miracle! It's so good to see you again!" She took in his whole appearance and frowned. "You have wings?"

Miracle smiled. "Yes. And you once knew me by another name, a very long time ago."

Velvet was confused. "At the Academy, you mean? But your name was Miracle? And you were an Oracle, not an Angel." She looked at Gold. "What is going on?"

Miracle held out his hand. "I get the feeling that when you take this, it will all become clear." He opened his hand to reveal a simple, worn wooden pendant on a leather string, resting on his palm.

Velvet didn't think she had ever seen it before, but it looked so very familiar at the same time. She reached out to take it, and when her fingers closed around the smooth rune, she felt as though she had been thrown into a kaleidoscope, as every memory from every timeline, from every lifetime, flashed before her, almost too fast to comprehend. When it finished, she doubled over, gasping for breath, feeling as though the very core of her being had been reshaped into something entirely new. When she could breathe again, she straightened up and looked down at the rune.

"Laguz," she whispered. She looked up at her friends. "Where is he?"

The Angel, whose name she now remembered was

Mica, smiled. "Laguz said that the necklace would lead you to him. I promised him that I would make sure you went straight there."

"When did you last see him?" Velvet asked, still a little breathless.

"At the Academy during the last timeline. He came looking for you, and we asked him not to interfere, because it would have meant that the Flames would have reunited, and the Diamond Age would not have happened."

Tears streamed down Velvet's cheeks. She wanted to ask more questions, she wanted to know why the timelines were changed, why the Flames were not meant to reunite, but none of that mattered quite as much as her Flame in that moment. "He's been waiting all this time?"

"Yes. Go to him."

Velvet nodded, and after encouraging smiles from Gold and Starlight, she closed her eyes, and asked the pendant to take her to him. Before she could open her eyes, a salty breeze washed over her and cold water lapped at her toes. She opened her eyes and looked down to see the waves soaking into her purple velvet robes. She looked up and down the golden beach, and smiled. He was near, she could feel it. She turned around and saw a very familiar house. It was the same as their home in Atlantis. She lifted her robes and walked as fast as she could up the beach. Her feet sunk into the soft sand, but it only slowed her down slightly.

With every step, she could feel all the many years slip away, and by the time she reached the house, her hair was glossy and dark, and her face was as youthful as during her life in Atlantis.

The soft notes of a piano reached her ears, and a hundred more memories crashed over her, making her close her eyes for moment. She let go of her robes, and pushed the door open. The sound of the piano got louder, and with tears falling slowly down her cheeks, Velvet walked barefoot through the house, following her heart and her ears towards the music.

When she reached the glass-walled room that held the magnificent white grand piano, she paused and watched her Flame playing for a while. Her heart felt like it would burst from the love and happiness she felt in that moment.

When the last note was played, yet still lingered in the air, she spoke.

"I'm home, my love."

She saw him close his eyes, and a tear trickle down his cheek. Then he looked up at her and she rushed over to him. He gathered her in his arms, and she breathed in his familiar scent.

"I can't believe it's taken so long for us to be together," he said, pulling back a little to look into her eyes.

Velvet frowned and looked down at the rune necklace in her hand. "I'm sorry it took me so long to remember."

He put his finger to her lips. "Shh. It wasn't your fault. Besides, it doesn't matter, we're together now."

"But all that time that we lost, all that time we could have been together?"

Laguz shook his head. "Are we or are we not together right now?"

She smiled. "We are."

"Then we have lost nothing." He leaned down and kissed her. She lost herself in his embrace, tasting the salt of her own tears on his lips. He pulled back slightly and gazed into her eyes.

"I'll love you for eternity," Laguz said, his voice filled

with unwavering certainty.

Velvet blinked, and another distant memory resurfaced in her mind. She smiled up at him and whispered back:

"Our love will outlast eternity itself."

Dear Reader,

Thank you so much for reading the Earth Angel Series, I really do appreciate your dedication to my books so very much. It has been such an amazing journey, and I am so glad that you came along with me!

As an Independent Author, I am very much reliant on word of mouth to let people know about my books, so if you enjoyed the series, please do tell your friends! And if you are so inclined, please leave a review on Amazon. I read them all and they have inspired me and cheered me on throughout the last decade. Reviews also help other readers to find the series too.

If you enjoyed the books and don't want the adventures to end, you can join the online Earth Angel Training Academy (EarthAngelAcademy.co.uk) and you can get the Oracle Cards from my website (MichelleGordon.co.uk).

Thank you for your time, your love and your support,

Much love,
Michelle

x

GRATITUDE

I am so very thankful for those who have been with me from the very beginning of this journey, when I wrote the first book of the series in 2009. I am also thankful for all of the amazing souls I have come to know and love along the way. Writing these books has not been a solitary journey, it has been a beautiful collaboration with the most amazing Earth Angels an Old Soul could wish for.

As this series comes to a close, so does almost a decade of my life, during which I have experienced so much. The pain, fear and sadness was balanced with blissful joy, happiness, laughter and love, and as I move onto new adventures, I know that I will remember these times fondly, with no regrets.

All my love and gratitude to my soul sisters, you nurture, nourish and care for me, I love you: Sarah Rebecca Vine, Niki Gilbert, Lucja Fratczak-Kay, Kelly Draper, Tiffany Hathorn, Crystal Dawne, Rachael Barnwell, Alex Lane, Charlotte Tomkins, Claire Weeks, Shelley-Nicole Brookdale, Roberta Smart, Amanda Bigrell, Rebecca Williams, McKenna Johnson, Molly Silva, Stacey Foster, Anne Bull, Sarah Smith, Jess Bailey, and Lara Fellows.

I feel so much gratitude for my soul brothers, who protect, uplift and encourage me, I love you, Andrew Embling, Kenny John, George Hardwick, John Sands, Robert Tremblay, Mr Bee, Damien Cordell, Xander Holland, Adrian Incledon-Webber, Rhys Westbury, James John Malaniak, John Costick, and Ray Ball.

Patreon patrons, you amaze me with your generosity and support, I love you all. Thank you, Kariel Tejai, Callie Raphael, Rachel Miller, Amanda Bigrell, Ana Leon and Tiffany Hathorn.

So much love to my dedicated fans who love my books so much. And those who encourage me to write, even if they've never read a word! Laurie Huston, Helen Gordon, Rachel Miller, Anabela Da Costa, Rosa Ivy, Hannah Dix, Chip Jenkins, Marc Gordon, Annette Ecuyere, Annie Hartwright, Cerian, Lily Wanda Waugh, Buckso Dhillon-Woolley, Malinda Rose, Nova Wightman, Becci Ann, Meera Virk, Lesley George, Margaux Joy DeNador, Louise Sofia Weir, David Wetton, Philip James, Sharon Andrews, Jenni Riley, Trish Mclean, Victor Keegan, Vikki Elizabeth Finlay, Tracey & Steve Howell, Duane Brovan, Trish Mclean, Trisha & Bruce Barnes, Jacqueline Wigglesworth, Meera Virk, Lou Brister, Nicky Lee, Bonny Blue, Nikki Jewison, Tim Marrow, Liz and Roger, Llinos Thomas, Nick Singh and Victor Keegan.

So much gratitude to my step-dad, John Byrne, for all the support over the last twelve years, and for making my mum so happy.

My mum, Sally Byrne, is my Angel, and I know that without her support, unconditional love and hugs I wouldn't have made it this far. Thank you, Mum, for everything, but especially for the hexies!

My sister, Liz Gordon, really is the best alien ever, and I am so very thankful for all the help and love. Liz, your genius has made so much of this journey possible, thank you!

My best friend, Elizabeth Lockwood, you are my rock, my Angel, and you have been there from the beginning of this Earth Angel adventure, thank you so much for sticking with me until the end, and for all the editing and for keeping me sane.

And finally, thank you Jon, for being a part of this journey, and for helping me to discover my true self. I remember who you truly are, and I wish you all the best.

ABOUT THE AUTHOR

Michelle lives in the UK, when she's not flitting in and out of other realms. She is an avid crafter, and enjoys letterpress printing, knitting, sewing, crochet, photography and many other creative pursuits. She has so far written fifteen novels for adults, one for children, a poetry collection and a self-help book.

Please feel free to write a review of this book. Michelle loves to get direct feedback, so if you would like to contact her, please e-mail **theamethystangel@hotmail.co.uk** or keep up to date by following her blog – **TwinFlameBlog.com.** You can also follow her on Twitter **@themiraclemuse** or on Instagram **@michellegordonauthor**

To sign up to her mailing list, visit:

michellegordon.co.uk

BOOKS BY MICHELLE GORDON

WHERE'S MY F**KING UNICORN?

Are your bookshelves filled with self-help books, and yet your life feels empty? Do you keep following paths to enlightenment that lead to the same dead ends? You've read the books, attended the seminars and taken heed of every bit of advice going... but you're still waiting for your f**king unicorn to come along! Where's My F**king Unicorn? is a guide to life, creativity and happiness that offers a very different way forward.

Author, Michelle Gordon, explains why, in spite of all your best efforts, your life still doesn't live up to your vision of what it should be, and tells you exactly what you can do about it. In refreshingly down-to-earth language, she shows you how to harness all the self-knowledge you have gained from all those self-help books you've read, and actually start putting it to practical use.

Where's My F**king Unicorn? is published by *Ammonite Press* and is available online and in bookstores.

THE GIRL WHO LOVED TOO MUCH

What would you do if you suddenly found yourself in a different reality that was better for you, but not for those you loved?

Caru loves to make things. And collect things. And give gifts. She loves to print, sew, knit, paint. Her life is full of unfinished projects, yet devoid of financial stability and romance. Though she loves her life, she finds herself disappointing people and struggling to keep everyone happy.

So when Caru wishes life could be simpler, and then finds herself in a completely different world, where her life is easy, money is abundant, and her long-term boyfriend is the most fabulous cook, she can't quite believe her luck.

But will all her wishes come true? Or will the dream turn into a nightmare?

The Girl Who Loved Too Much is a modern day 'It's a Wonderful Life'.

The Girl Who Loved Too Much is published by *Jasper Tree Press* and is available online in eBook and print.

THE OLD SOUL'S HANDBOOK

It's not easy being an Earth Angel on this planet.
I hope the words within these pages help you in whatever
situation you find yourself in.
Simply ask a question or for guidance, and then open the
book to a random page.
The answers are within.

The Earth Angel Series is published by
The Amethyst Angel and is available online in eBook and print.

Not From This Planet is an Independent Publisher on a mission to collaborate with authors to create the best possible books that delight and inspire and entertain – and also pay a fair royalty to the author. They treat every book as if it were their own and they have big have plans to take the publishing world by storm.

Follow Not From This Planet on
Instagram - @notfromthisplanetbooks
Facebook - @notfromthisplanetbooks
Twitter - @ NFTPbooks

NotFromThisPlanet.co.uk

www.ingramcontent.com/pod-product-compliance
Lightning Source LLC
Chambersburg PA
CBHW071256190726
48292CB00007B/2567